New insights are offered to combat the stereotyped image of youth in these modern, seldom before anthologized stories by distinguished writers.

ROBERT S. GOLD is a member of the English Department at Jersey City State College and has taught at Queens College and New York University. He is the author of *A Jazz Lexicon*.

ALSO AVAILABLE IN LAUREL-LEAF BOOKS:

CONNECTIONS: SHORT STORIES BY OUTSTANDING
WRITERS FOR YOUNG ADULTS,
edited by Donald R. Gallo
SIXTEEN: SHORT STORIES BY OUTSTANDING WRITERS
FOR YOUNG ADULTS,
edited by Donald R. Gallo
VISIONS: NINETEEN SHORT STORIES BY OUTSTANDING
WRITERS FOR YOUNG ADULTS,
edited by Donald R. Gallo
THE CHOCOLATE WAR, *Robert Cormier*
BEYOND THE CHOCOLATE WAR, *Robert Cormier*
I AM THE CHEESE, *Robert Cormier*
THE BUMBLEBEE FLIES ANYWAY, *Robert Cormier*
EIGHT PLUS ONE, *Robert Cormier*
AFTER THE FIRST DEATH, *Robert Cormier*
TALK TO ME: SHORT STORIES AND A NOVELLA,
Carol Dines

Point of Departure

19 STORIES OF YOUTH AND DISCOVERY

EDITED BY

Robert S. Gold

Published by
Bantam Doubleday Dell Books for Young Readers
a division of
Bantam Doubleday Dell Publishing Group, Inc.
1540 Broadway
New York, New York 10036

ISBN: 0-440-96983-2

RL: 6.0

Printed in the United States of America
One Previous Dell Edition
New Dell Edition
February 1981

43 42

RAD

ACKNOWLEDGMENTS

*The following stories are reprinted by permission of the authors,
agents and publisher:*

"The Wishing Well" by Phillip Bonosky: Copyright 1949 in the
United States and Great Britain by Masses and Mainstream
Inc. Reprinted by permission of New Era Book and Subscrip-
tion Agency.
"The White Circle" by John Bell Clayton: Copyright 1947 by
John Bell Clayton. First published in *Harper's Magazine*. Re-
printed by permission of Toni Strassman, Author's Represen-
tative.

CONTENTS

INTRODUCTION

ADOLESCENCE has never had a good press. "Unmannerly and disobedient" were the charges hurled at the youth of Athens 2,500 years ago by no less an authority than Socrates (who, ironically, was considered quite a cut-up by *his* social superiors).

While Socrates' complaint echoes and reechoes through the ages with surprisingly little variation, counter-arguments have rarely been heard. Like all minority groups, adolescents are too busy just trying to live and, besides, have too little power to combat the adult majority's view of them—i.e., that they are indolent, disrespectful, slovenly and rebellious; that their clothes are too casual, their hair too long (or too short, depending on the historical period), their speech too slangy; and that, generally, they are lacking in the traditional virtues (whatever these might be). Like all stereotypes, this one dies hard.

As any thoughtful person knows, the only safe generalization to be made about adolescence is that it's a very trying, frequently anguished stage of life, with seemingly endless twists and variations in the *ways* it can be difficult.

In this collection of stories are registered some of the range and scope of adolescent experience—the pain and confusion and excitement and discovery—and, incidentally, a corrective is offered to the false public image of *one kind* of adolescence or *one kind* of adolescent.

Look, for example, at the multiple effects of class distinctions suggested by Alan Sillitoe's "The Bike," Jesse Stuart's "Split Cherry Tree," John Bell Clayton's "The

White Circle and Phillip Bonosky's "The Wishing Well"; at how race and religion can complicate poverty in Paul Laurence Dunbar's "The Finish of Patsy Barnes," William Melvin Kelley's "A Good Long Sidewalk" and Albert Halper's horrifyingly prophetic "Prelude."

Look, too, at what is discovered, or uncovered, about the foibles of adults in John Updike's "A & P," Berton Roueché's "Phone Call" and Kelley's story; and at the variety of universal experiences revealed in Elizabeth Taylor's "The First Death of Her Life," Nadine Gordimer's "A Company of Laughing Faces," Elizabeth Enright's "The Eclipse," Saroyan's "Seventeen," Malamud's "A Summer's Reading" and Carson McCuller's "Sucker."

Look, finally, at the different *levels* of experience among Ben Hecht's "Snowfall in Childhood," Howard Nemerov's fantasy "The Sorcerer's Eye," John Updike's "Tomorrow and Tomorrow and So Forth," and John Collier's outrageously funny "Ah, the University."

Here, then, in these nineteen stories is the varied, irreducible world of adolescence.

ROBERT S. GOLD

THE BIKE

by Alan Sillitoe

THE EASTER I WAS FIFTEEN I sat at the table for supper and Mam said to me: "I'm glad you've left school. Now you can go to work."

"I don't want to go to wok," I said in a big voice.

"Well, you've got to," she said. "I can't afford to keep a pit-prop like yo' on nowt."

I sulked, pushed my toasted cheese away as if it was the worst kind of slop. "I thought I could have a break before starting."

"Well you thought wrong. You'll be out of harm's way at work." She took my plate and emptied it on John's, my younger brother's, knowing the right way to get me mad. That's the trouble with me: I'm not clever. I could have bashed our John's face in and snatched it back, except the little bastard had gobbled it up, and Dad was sitting by the fire, behind his paper with one tab lifted. "You can't get me out to wok quick enough, can you?" was all I could say to Mam.

Dad chipped in, put down his paper. "Listen: no wok, no grub. So get out and look for a job tomorrow, and don't come back till you've got one."

Going to the bike factory to ask for a job meant getting up early, just as if I was back at school; there didn't seem any point in getting older. My old man was a good worker though, and I knew in my bones and brain that I took after him. At the school garden the teacher used to say: "Colin, you're the best worker I've got, and you'll get on when you leave"—after I'd spent a couple of hours digging spuds while all the others had been larking about trying to run each other over with the lawn-rollers. Then the teacher would sell the spuds off at threepence a pound and what did I get out of it? Bogger-all. Yet I liked the work because it wore me out; and I always feel pretty good when I'm worn out.

I knew you had to go to work though, and that rough work was best. I saw a picture once about a revolution in Russia, about the workers taking over everything (like Dad wants to) and they lined everybody up and made them hold their hands out and the working blokes went up and down looking at them. Anybody whose hands was lily-white was taken away and shot. The others was O.K. Well, if ever that happened in this country, I'd be O.K., and that made me feel better when a few days later I was walking down the street in overalls at half-past seven in the morning with the rest of them. One side of my face felt lively and interested in what I was in for, but the other side was crooked and sorry for itself, so that a neighbour got a front view of my whole clock and called with a wide laugh, a gap I'd like to have seen a few inches lower down—in her neck: "Never mind, Colin, it ain't all that bad."

The man on the gate took me to the turnery. The noise hit me like a boxing-glove as I went in, but I kept on walking straight into it without flinching, feeling it reach right into my guts as if to wrench them out and use them as garters. I was handed over to the foreman; then the foreman passed me on to the toolsetter; and the toolsetter took me to another youth—so that I began to feel like a hot wallet.

The youth led me to a cupboard, opened it, and gave me a sweeping brush. "Yo' do that gangway," he said, "and I'll do this one." My gangway was wider, but I didn't bother to mention it. "Bernard," he said, holding out his hand, "that's me. I go on a machine next week, a drill."

"How long you been on this sweeping?" I wanted to know, bored with it already.

"Three months. Every lad gets put on sweeping first, just to get 'em used to the place." Bernard was small and thin, older than me. We took to each other. He had round

bright eyes and dark wavy hair, and spoke in a quick way
as if he'd stayed at school longer than he had. He was idle,
and I thought him sharp and clever, maybe because his
mam and dad died when he was three. He'd been brought
up by an asthmatic auntie who'd not only spoiled him but
let him run wild as well, he told me later when we sat sup-
ping from our tea mugs. He'd quietened down now though,
and butter wouldn't melt in his mouth, he said with a
wink. I couldn't think why this was, after all his stories
about him being a mad-head—which put me off him at
first, though after a bit he was my mate, and that was that.

We was talking one day, and Bernard said the thing he
wanted to buy most in the world was a gram and lots of
jazz records—New Orleans style. He was saving up and
had already got ten quid.

"Me," I said, "I want a bike, to get out at week ends
up Trent. A shop on Arkwright Street sells good 'uns
second hand."

I went back to my sweeping. It was a fact I've always
wanted a bike. Speed gave me a thrill. Malcolm Campbell
was my bigshot—but I'd settle for a two-wheeled pushbike.
I'd once borrowed my cousin's and gone down Balloon
House Hill so quick I passed a bus. I'd often thought how
easy it would be to pinch a bike: look in a shop window
until a bloke leaves his bike to go into the same shop, then
nip in just before him and ask for something you knew
they hadn't got; then walk out whistling to the bike at
the curb and ride off as if it's yours while the bloke's still
in the shop. I'd brood for hours: fly home on it, enamel it,
file off the numbers, turn the handlebars round, change the
pedals, take lamps off or put them on . . . only, no, I
thought, I'll be honest and save up for one when I get
forced out to work, worse luck.

But work turned out to be a better life than school. I
kept as hard at it as I could, and got on well with the blokes
because I used to spout about how rotten the wages was
and how hard the bosses slaved us—which made me
popular you can bet. Like my old man always says, I told
them: "At home, when you've got a headache, mash a

pot of tea. At work, when you've got a headache, strike."
Which brought a few laughs.

Bernard was put on his drill, and one Friday while he
was cleaning it down I stood waiting to cart his rammel
off. "Are you still saving up for that bike, then?" he
asked, pushing steel dust away with a handbrush.

"Course I am. But I'm a way off getting one yet. They
rush you a fiver at that shop. Guaranteed, though."

He worked on for a minute or two then, as if he'd got a
birthday present or was trying to spring a good surprise
on me, said without turning round: "I've made up my
mind to sell my bike."

"I didn't know you'd got one."

"Well"—a look on his face as if there was a few things
I didn't know—"I bus it to work: it's easier." Then in a
pallier voice: "I got it last Christmas, from my auntie. But
I want a record player now."

My heart was thumping. I knew I hadn't got enough,
but: "How much do you want for it?"

He smiled. "It ain't how much I want for the bike, it's
how much more dough I need to get the gram and a couple
of discs."

I saw Trent Valley spread out below me from the top of
Carlton Hill—fields and villages, and the river like a white
scarf dropped from a giant's neck. "How much do you
need, then?"

He took his time about it, as if still having to reckon it
up. "Fifty bob." I'd only got two quid—so the giant
snatched his scarf away and vanished. Then Bernard seemed
in a hurry to finish the deal: "Look, I don't want to mess
about, I'll let it go for two pounds five. You can borrow the
other five bob."

"I'll do it then," I said, and Bernard shook my hand like
he was going away in the army. "It's a deal. Bring the
dough in the morning, and I'll bike it to wok."

Dad was already in when I got home, filling the kettle
at the scullery tap. I don't think he felt safe without there
was a kettle on the gas. "What would you do if the world

suddenly ended, Dad?" I once asked when he was in a good mood. "Mash some tea and watch it," he said. He poured me a cup.

"Lend's five bob, Dad, till Friday."

He slipped the cosy on. "What do you want to borrow money for?" I told him. "Who from?" he asked.

"My mate at wok."

He passed me the money. "Is it a good 'un?"

"I ain't seen it yet. He's bringing it in the morning."

"Make sure the brakes is safe."

Bernard came in half an hour late, so I wasn't able to see the bike till dinner-time. I kept thinking he'd took bad and wouldn't come at all, but suddenly he was stooping at the door to take his clips off—so's I'd know he'd got his—my—bike. He looked paler than usual, as if he'd been up the canal-bank all night with a piece of skirt and caught a bilious-bout. I paid him at dinner-time. "Do you want a receipt for it?" he laughed. It was no time to lark about. I gave it a short test around the factory, then rode it home.

The next three evenings, for it was well in to summer, I rode a dozen miles out into the country, where fresh air smelt like cowshit and the land was coloured different, was wide open and windier than in streets. Marvellous. It was like a new life starting up, as if till then I'd been tied by a mile-long rope round the ankle to home. Whistling along lanes I planned trips to Skegness, wondering how many miles I could make in a whole day. If I pedalled like mad, bursting my lungs for fifteen hours I'd reach London where I'd never been. It was like sawing through the bars in clink. It was a good bike as well, a few years old, but a smart racer with lamps and saddlebags and a pump that went. I thought Bernard was a bit loony parting with it at that price, but I supposed that that's how blokes are when they get dead set on a gram and discs. They'd sell their own mother, I thought, enjoying a mad dash down from Canning Circus, weaving between the cars for kicks.

"What's it like, having a bike?" Bernard asked, stopping to slap me on the back—as jolly as I'd ever seen him, yet in a kind of way that don't happen between pals.

"You should know," I said. "Why? It's all right, ain't it? The wheels are good, aren't they?"

An insulted look came into his eyes. "You can give it back if you like. I'll give you your money."

"I don't want it," I said. I could no more part with it than my right arm, and he knew it. "Got the gram yet?" And he told me about it for the next half-hour. It had got so many dials for this and that he made it sound like a space ship. We was both satisfied, which was the main thing.

That same Saturday I went to the barber's for my monthly D.A. and when I came out I saw a bloke getting on my bike to ride it away. I tagged him on the shoulder, my fist flashing red for danger.

"Off," I said sharp, ready to smash the thieving bastard. He turned to me. A funny sort of thief, I couldn't help thinking, a respectable-looking bloke of about forty wearing glasses and shiny shoes, smaller than me, with a moustache. Still, the swivel-eyed sinner was taking my bike.

"I'm boggered if I will," he said, in a quiet way so that I thought he was a bit touched. "It's my bike, anyway."

"It bloody-well ain't," I swore, "and if you don't get off I'll crack you one."

A few people gawked at us. The bloke didn't mess about and I can understand it now. "Missis," he called, "just go down the road to that copperbox and ask a policeman to come up 'ere, will you? This is my bike, and this young bogger nicked it."

I was strong for my age. "You sodding fibber," I cried, pulling him clean off the bike so's it clattered to the pavement. I picked it up to ride away, but the bloke got me round the waist, and it was more than I could do to take him off up the road as well, even if I wanted to. Which I didn't.

"Fancy robbing a working-man of his bike," somebody called out from the crowd of idle bastards now collected. I could have mowed them down.

But I didn't get a chance. A copper came, and the man

was soon flicking out his wallet, showing a bill with the number of the bike on it: proof right enough. But I still thought he'd made a mistake. "You can tell us all about that at the Guildhall," the copper said to me.

I don't know why—I suppose I want my brains tested —but I stuck to a story that I found the bike dumped at the end of the yard that morning and was on my way to give it in at a copshop, and had called for a haircut first. I think the magistrate half believed me, because the bloke knew to the minute when it was pinched, and at that time I had a perfect alibi—I was in work, proved by my clocking-in card. I knew some rat who hadn't been in work though when he should have been.

All the same, being found with a pinched bike, I got put on probation, and am still doing it. I hate old Bernard's guts for playing a trick like that on me, his mate. But it was lucky for him I hated the coppers more and wouldn't squeal on anybody, not even a dog. Dad would have killed me if ever I had, though he didn't need to tell me. I could only thank God a story came to me as quick as it did, though in one way I still sometimes reckon I was barmy not to have told them how I got that bike.

There's one thing I do know. I'm waiting for Bernard to come out of reform school. He got picked up, the day after I was copped with the bike, for robbing his auntie's gas meter to buy more discs. She'd had about all she could stand from him, and thought a spell inside would do him good, if not cure him altogether. I've got a big bone to pick with him, because he owes me forty-five bob. I don't care where he gets it—even if he goes out and robs another meter—but I'll get it out of him, I swear blind I will. I'll pulverise him.

Another thing about him though that makes me laugh is that, if ever there's a revolution and everybody's lined up with their hands out, Bernard's will still be lily-white, because he's a bone-idle thieving bastard—and then we'll see how he goes on; because mine won't be lily-white, I can tell you that now. And you never know, I might even be one of the blokes picking 'em out.

SPLIT CHERRY TREE

by Jesse Stuart

I DON'T MIND staying after school," I says to Professor Herbert, "but I'd rather you'd whip me with a switch and let me go home early. Pa will whip me anyway for getting home two hours late."

"You are too big to whip," says Professor Herbert, "and I have to punish you for climbing up in the cherry tree. You boys knew better than that! The other five boys have paid their dollar each. You have been the only one who has not helped pay for the tree. Can't you borrow a dollar?"

"I can't," I says. "I'll have to take the punishment. I wish it would be quicker punishment. I wouldn't mind."

Professor Herbert stood and looked at me. He was a big man. He wore a gray suit of clothes. The suit matched his gray hair.

"You don't know my father," I says to Professor Herbert. "He might be called a little old-fashioned. He makes us mind him until we're twenty-one years old. He believes: 'If you spare the rod you spoil the child.' I'll never be able to make him understand about the cherry tree. I'm the first of my people to go to high school."

"You must take the punishment," says Professor Herbert. "You must stay two hours after school today and two hours after school tomorrow. I am allowing you twenty-five cents an hour. That is good money for a high school student. You can sweep the schoolhouse floor, wash the blackboards and clean windows. I'll pay the dollar for you."

I couldn't ask Professor Herbert to loan me a dollar.

He never offered to loan it to me. I had to stay and help the janitor and work out my fine at a quarter an hour.

I thought as I swept the floor: "What will Pa do to me? What lie can I tell him when I go home? Why did we ever climb that cherry tree and break it down for anyway? Why did we run crazy over the hills away from the crowd? Why did we do all of this? Six of us climbed up in a little cherry tree after one little lizard! Why did the tree split and fall with us? It should have been a stronger tree! Why did Eif Crabtree just happen to be below us plowing and catch us in his cherry tree? Why wasn't he a better man than to charge us six dollars for the tree?"

It was six o'clock when I left the schoolhouse. I had six miles to walk home. It would be after seven when I got home. I had all my work to do when I got home. It took Pa and me both to do the work. Seven cows to milk. Nineteen head of cattle to feed, four mules, twenty-five hogs. Firewood and stovewood to cut and water to draw from the well. He would be doing it when I got home. He would be mad and wondering what was keeping me!

I hurried home. I would run under the dark leafless trees. I would walk fast uphill. I would run down the hill. The ground was freezing. I had to hurry. I had to run. I reached the long ridge that led to our cow pasture. I ran along this ridge. The wind dried the sweat on my face. I ran across the pasture to the house.

I threw down my books in the chipyard. I ran to the barn to spread fodder on the ground for the cattle. I didn't take time to change my clean school clothes for my old work clothes. I ran out to the barn. I saw Pa spreading fodder on the ground to the cattle. That was my job. I ran up to the fence. I says: "Leave that for me, Pa. I'll do it. I'm just a little late."

"I see you are," says Pa. He turned and looked at me. His eyes danced fire. "What in th' world has kept you so? Why ain't you been here to help me with this work? Make a gentleman out'n one boy in th' family and this is what you get! Send you to high school and you get too onery fer th' buzzards to smell!"

I never said anything. I didn't want to tell why I was late from school. Pa stopped scattering the bundles of fodder. He looked at me. He says: "Why are you gettin' in here this time o' night? You tell me or I'll take a hickory withe to you right here on th' spot!"

I says: "I had to stay after school." I couldn't lie to Pa. He'd go to school and find out why I had to stay. If I lied to him it would be too bad for me.

"Why did you haf to stay atter school?" says Pa.

I says: "Our biology class went on a field trip today. Six of us boys broke down a cherry tree. We had to give a dollar apiece to pay for the tree. I didn't have the dollar. Professor Herbert is making me work out my dollar. He gives me twenty-five cents an hour. I had to stay in this afternoon. I'll have to stay in tomorrow afternoon!"

"Are you telling me th' truth?" says Pa.

"I'm telling you the truth," I says. "Go and see for yourself."

"That's just what I'll do in th' mornin'," says Pa. "Jist whose cherry tree did you break down?"

"Eif Crabtree's cherry tree!"

"What was you doin' clear out in Eif Crabtree's place?" says Pa. "He lives four miles from th' County High School. Don't they teach you no books at that high school? Do they jist let you get out and gad over th' hillsides? If that's all they do I'll keep you at home, Dave. I've got work here fer you to do!"

"Pa," I says, "spring is just getting here. We take a subject in school where we have to have bugs, snakes, flowers, lizards, frogs and plants. It is biology. It was a pretty day today. We went out to find a few of these. Six of us boys saw a lizard at the same time sunning on a cherry tree. We all went up the tree to get it. We broke the tree down. It split at the forks. Eif Crabtree was plowing down below us. He ran up the hill and got our names. The other boys gave their dollar apiece. I didn't have mine. Professor Herbert put mine in for me. I have to work it out at school."

"Poor man's son, huh," says Pa. "I'll attend to that myself in th' mornin'. I'll take keer o' 'im. He ain't from this country nohow. I'll go down there in th' mornin' and see 'im. Lettin' you leave your books and galavant all over th' hills. What kind of a school is it nohow! Didn't do that, my son, when I's a little shaver in school. All fared alike too."

"Pa, please don't go down there," I says. "Just let me have fifty cents and pay the rest of my fine. I don't want you to go down there! I don't want you to start anything with Professor Herbert!"

"Ashamed of your old Pap, are you, Dave," says Pa, "atter the way I've worked to raise you! Tryin' to send you to school so you can make a better livin' than I've made."

I thought once I'd run through the woods above the barn just as hard as I could go. I thought I'd leave high school and home forever! Pa could not catch me! I'd get away! I couldn't go back to school with him. He'd have a gun and maybe he'd shoot Professor Herbert. It was hard to tell what he would do. I could tell Pa that school had changed in the hills from the way it was when he was a boy, but he wouldn't understand. I could tell him we studied frogs, birds, snakes, lizards, flowers, insects. But Pa wouldn't understand. If I did run away from home it wouldn't matter to Pa. He would see Professor Herbert anyway. He would think that high school and Professor Herbert had run me away from home. There was no need to run away. I'd just have to stay, finish foddering the cattle and go to school with Pa the next morning.

The moon shone bright in the cold March sky. I finished my work by moonlight. Professor Herbert really didn't know how much work I had to do at home. If he had known he would not have kept me after school. He would have loaned me a dollar to have paid my part on the cherry tree. He had never lived in the hills. He didn't know the way the hill boys had to work so that they could go to school. Now he was teaching in a County High School where all the boys who attended were from hill farms.

After I'd finished doing my work I went to the house and ate my supper. Pa and Mom had eaten. My supper was getting cold. I heard Pa and Mom talking in the front room. Pa was telling Mom about me staying in after school.

"I had to do all th' milkin' tonight, chop th' wood myself. It's too hard on me atter I've turned ground all day. I'm goin' to take a day off tomorrow and see if I can't remedy things a little. I'll go down to the high school tomorrow. I won't be a very good scholar fer Professor Herbert nohow. He won't keep me in atter school. I'll take a different kind of lesson down there and make 'im acquainted with it."

"Now, Luster," says Mom, "you jist stay away from there. Don't cause a lot o' trouble. You can be jailed fer a trick like that. You'll get th' Law atter you. You'll jist go down there and show off and plague your own boy Dave to death in front o' all th' scholars!"

"Plague or no plague," says Pa, "he don't take into consideration what all I haf to do here, does he? I'll show 'im it ain't right to keep one boy in and let the rest go scot-free. My boy is good as th' rest, ain't he? A bullet will make a hole in a schoolteacher same as it will anybody else. He can't do me that way and get by with it. I'll plug 'im first. I aim to go down there bright and early in th' mornin' and get all this straight! I aim to see about bug learnin' and this runnin' all over God's creation huntin' snakes, lizards, and frogs. Ransackin' th' country and goin' through cherry orchards and breakin' th' trees down atter lizards! Old Eif Crabtree ought to a-poured th' hot lead into 'em instead o' chargin' six dollars fer th' tree! He ought to a-got old Herbert the first one!"

I ate my supper. I slipped upstairs and lit the lamp. I tried to forget the whole thing. I studied plane geometry. Then I studied my biology lesson. I could hardly study for thinking about Pa. "He'll go to school with me in the morning. He'll take a gun for Professor Herbert! What will Professor Herbert think of me! I'll tell him when Pa leaves that I couldn't help it. But Pa might shoot him. I hate to go with Pa. Maybe he'll cool off about it tonight and not go in the morning."

Pa got up at four o'clock. He built a fire in the stove. Then he built a fire in the fireplace. He got Mom up to get breakfast. Then he got me up to help feed and milk. By the time we had our work done at the barn, Mom had breakfast ready for us. We ate our breakfast. Daylight came and we could see the bare oak trees covered white with frost. The hills were white with frost.

"Now, Dave," says Pa, "let's get ready fer school. I aim to go with you this mornin' and look into bug larnin', frog larnin', lizard and snake larnin' and breakin' down cherry trees! I don't like no sicha foolish way o' larnin' myself!"

Pa hadn't forgot. I'd have to take him to school with me. He would take me to school with him. I was glad we were going early. If Pa pulled a gun on Professor Herbert there wouldn't be so many of my classmates there to see him.

I knew that Pa wouldn't be at home in the high school. He wore overalls, big boots, a blue shirt and a sheepskin coat and a slouched black hat gone to seed at the top. He put his gun in its holster. We started trudging toward the high school across the hill.

It was early when we got to the County High School. Professor Herbert had just got there. I just thought as we walked up the steps into the schoolhouse: "Maybe Pa will find out Professor Herbert is a good man. He just doesn't know him. Just like I felt toward the Lambert boys across the hill. I didn't like them until I'd seen them and talked to them, then I liked them and we were friends. It's a lot in knowing the other fellow."

"You're th' Professor here, ain't you?" says Pa.

"Yes," says Professor Herbert, "and you are Dave's father?"

"Yes," says Pa, pulling out his gun and laying it on the seat in Professor Herbert's office. Professor Herbert's eyes got big behind his black-rimmed glasses when he saw Pa's gun. Color came into his pale cheeks.

"Jist a few things about this school I want to know," says Pa. "I'm tryin' to make a scholar out'n Dave. He's the only one out'n eleven youngins I've sent to high school. Here he comes in late and leaves me all th' work to do! He said you's all out bug huntin' yesterday and broke a cherry tree down. He had to stay two hours atter school yesterday and work out money to pay on that cherry tree! Is that right?"

"W-w-why," says Professor Herbert, "I guess it is."

He looked at Pa's gun.

"Well," says Pa, "this ain't no high school. It's a damn bug school, a lizard school, a snake school! It ain't no damn school nohow!"

"Why did you bring that gun?" says Professor Herbert to Pa.

"You see that little hole," says Pa as he picked up the long blue forty-four and put his finger on the end of the barrel. "A bullet can come out'n that hole that will kill a schoolteacher same as it will any other man. It will kill a rich man same as a poor man. It will kill a man. But atter I come in and saw you, I know'd I wouldn't need it. This maul o' mine could do you up in a few minutes."

Pa stood there, big, hard, brown-skinned and mighty beside of Professor Herbert. I didn't know Pa was so much bigger and harder. I'd never seen Pa in a schoolhouse before. I'd seen Professor Herbert. He always looked big before to me. He didn't look big standing beside of Pa.

"I was only doing my duty," says Professor Herbert, "Mr. Sexton, and following the course of study the state provided us with."

"Course o' study!" says Pa. "What study? Bug study? Varmint study? Takin' youngins to th' woods. Boys and girls all out there together a-galavantin' in the brush and kickin' up their heels and their poor old Mas and Pas at home a-slavin' to keep 'em in school and give 'em a education!"

Students are coming into the schoolhouse now. Professor Herbert says: "Close the door, Dave, so others won't hear."

I walked over and closed the door. I was shaking like a leaf in the wind. I thought Pa was going to hit Professor Herbert every minute. He was doing all the talking. His face was getting red. The red color was coming through the brown, weather-beaten skin on Pa's face.

"It jist don't look good to me," says Pa, "a-takin' all this swarm of youngins out to pillage th' whole deestrict. Breakin' down cherry trees. Keepin' boys in atter school."

"What else could I have done with Dave, Mr. Sexton?" says Professor Herbert. "The boys didn't have any business all climbing that cherry tree after one lizard. One boy could have gone up the tree and got it. The farmer charged us six dollars. It was a little steep, I think, but we had it to pay. Must I make five boys pay and let your boy off? He said he didn't have the dollar and couldn't get it. So I put it in for him. I'm letting him work it out. He's not working for me. He's working for the school!"

"I jist don't know what you could a-done with 'im," says Pa, "only a-larruped 'im with a withe! That's what he needed!"

"He's too big to whip," says Professor Herbert, pointing at me. "He's a man in size."

"He's not too big fer me to whip," says Pa. "They ain't too big until they're over twenty-one! It jist didn't look fair to me! Work one and let th' rest out because they got th' money. I don't see what bugs has got to do with a high school! It don't look good to me nohow!"

Pa picked up his gun and put it back in its holster. The red color left Professor Herbert's face. He talked more to Pa. Pa softened a little. It looked funny to see Pa in the high school building. It was the first time he'd ever been there.

"We're not only hunting snakes, toads, flowers, butterflies, lizards," says Professor Herbert, "but, Mr. Sexton, I was hunting dry timothy grass to put in an incubator and raise some protozoa."

"I don't know what that is," says Pa. "Th' incubator is th' new-fangled way o' cheatin' th' hens and raisin' chickens. I ain't so sure about th' breed o' chickens you mentioned."

"You've heard of germs, Mr. Sexton, haven't you?" says Professor Herbert.

"Jist call me Luster if you don't mind," says Pa, very casual like.

"All right, Luster, you've heard of germs, haven't you?"

"Yes," says Pa, "but I don't believe in germs. I'm sixty-five years old and I ain't seen one yet!"

"You can't see them with your naked eye," says Professor Herbert. "Just keep that gun in the holster and stay with me in the high school today. I have a few things I want to show you. That scum on your teeth has germs in it."

"What," says Pa, "you mean to tell me I've got germs on my teeth!"

"Yes," says Professor Herbert. "The same kind as we might be able to find in a living black snake if we dissect it!"

"I don't mean to dispute your word," says Pa, "but damned if I believe it. I don't believe I have germs on my teeth!"

"Stay with me today and I'll show you. I want to take you through the school anyway. School has changed a lot in the hills since you went to school. I don't guess we had high schools in this county when you went to school."

"No," says Pa, "jist readin', writin' and cipherin'. We didn't have all this bug larnin', and findin' germs on your teeth and in the middle o' black snakes! Th' world's changin'."

"It is," says Professor Herbert, "and we hope all for the better. Boys like your own there are going to help change it. He's your boy. He knows all of what I've told you. You stay with me today."

"I'll shore stay with you," says Pa. "I want to see th' germs off'n my teeth. I jist want to see a germ. I've never seen one in my life. 'Seein' is believin',' Pap allus told me."

Pa walks out of the office with Professor Herbert. I just hoped Professor Herbert didn't have Pa arrested for pulling his gun. Pa's gun has always been a friend to him when he goes to settle disputes.

The bell rang. School took up. I saw the students when they marched in the schoolhouse look at Pa. They would grin and punch each other. Pa just stood and watched them pass in at the schoolhouse door. Two long lines marched in the house. The boys and girls were clean and well dressed. Pa stood over in the schoolyard under a leafless elm, in his sheepskin coat, his big boots laced in front with buckskin and his heavy socks stuck above his boot tops. Pa's overalls legs were baggy and wrinkled between his coat and boot tops. His blue work shirt showed at the collar. His big black hat showed his gray-streaked black hair. His face was hard and weathertanned to the color of a ripe fodder blade. His hands were big and gnarled like the roots of the elm tree he stood beside.

When I went to my first class I saw Pa and Professor Herbert going around over the schoolhouse. I was in my geometry class when Pa and Professor Herbert came in the room. We were explaining our propositions on the blackboard. Professor Herbert and Pa just quietly came in and sat down awhile. I heard Fred Wurts whisper to Glenn Armstrong: "Who is that old man? Lord, he's a rough-looking scamp." Glenn whispered back: "I think he's Dave's Pap." The students in geometry looked at Pa. They must have wondered what he was doing in school. Before the class was over, Pa and Professor Herbert got up and went out. I saw them together down on the playground. Professor Herbert was explaining to Pa. I could see the outline of Pa's gun under his coat when he'd walk around.

At noon in the high school cafeteria Pa and Professor Herbert sat together at the little table where Professor Herbert always ate by himself. They ate together. The students watched the way Pa ate. He ate with his knife instead of his fork. A lot of the students felt sorry for me after they found out he was my father. They didn't have to feel sorry for me. I wasn't ashamed of Pa after I found out he wasn't going to shoot Professor Herbert. I was glad they had made friends. I wasn't ashamed of Pa. I wouldn't be as long as he behaved.

In the afternoon when we went to biology Pa was in the class. He was sitting on one of the high stools beside the microscope. We went ahead with our work just as if Pa wasn't in the class. I saw Pa take his knife and scrape tartar from one of his teeth. Professor Herbert put it under the lens and adjusted the microscope for Pa. He adjusted it and worked awhile. Then he says: "Now, Luster, look! Put your eye right down to the light. Squint the other eye!"

Pa put his head down and did as Professor Herbert said: "I see 'im," says Pa. "Who'd a ever thought that? Right on a body's teeth! Right in a body's mouth! You're right certain they ain't no fake to this, Professor Herbert?"

"No, Luster," says Professor Herbert. "It's there. That's the germ. Germs live in a world we cannot see with the naked eye. We must use the microscope. There are millions of them in our bodies. Some are harmful. Others are helpful."

Pa holds his face down and looks through the microscope. We stop and watch Pa. He sits upon the tall stool. His knees are against the table. His legs are long. His coat slips up behind when he bends over. The handle of his gun shows. Professor Herbert quickly pulls his coat down.

"Oh, yes," says Pa. He gets up and pulls his coat down. Pa's face gets a little red. He knows about his gun and he knows he doesn't have any use for it in high school.

"We have a big black snake over here we caught yesterday," says Professor Herbert. "We'll chloroform him and dissect him and show you he has germs in his body too."

"Don't do it," says Pa. "I believe you. I jist don't want to see you kill the black snake. I never kill one. They are good mousers and a lot o' help to us on the farm. I like black snakes. I jist hate to see people kill 'em. I don't allow 'em killed on my place."

The students look at Pa. They seem to like him better after he said that. Pa with a gun in his pocket but a tender heart beneath his ribs for snakes, but not for man! Pa won't whip a mule at home. He won't whip his cattle.

Professor Herbert took Pa through the laboratory. He showed him the different kinds of work we were doing. He showed him our equipment. They stood and talked while we worked. Then they walked out together. They talked louder when they got out in the hall.

When our biology class was over I walked out of the room. It was our last class for the day. I would have to take my broom and sweep two hours to finish paying for the split cherry tree. I just wondered if Pa would want me to stay. He was standing in the hallway watching the students march out. He looked lost among us. He looked like a leaf turned brown on the tree among the tree top filled with growing leaves.

I got my broom and started to sweep. Professor Herbert walked up and says: "I'm going to let you do that some other time. You can go home with your father. He is waiting out there."

I laid my broom down, got my books, and went down the steps.

Pa says: "Ain't you got two hours o' sweepin' yet to do?"

I says: "Professor Herbert said I could do it some other time. He said for me to go home with you."

"No," says Pa. "You are goin' to do as he says. He's a good man. School has changed from my day and time. I'm a dead leaf, Dave. I'm behind. I don't belong here. If he'll let me I'll get a broom and we'll both sweep one hour. That pays your debt. I'll help you pay it. I'll ast 'im and see if he won't let me hep you."

"I'm going to cancel the debt," says Professor Herbert. "I just wanted you to understand, Luster."

"I understand," says Pa, "and since I understand he must pay his debt fer th' tree and I'm goin' to hep him."

"Don't do that," says Professor Herbert. "It's all on me."

"We don't do things like that," says Pa; "we're just and honest people. We don't want somethin' fer nothin'. Professor Herbert, you're wrong now and I'm right. You'll haf to listen to me. I've learned a lot from you. My boy must go on. Th' world has left me. It changed while I've raised my family and plowed th' hills. I'm a just and honest man. I don't skip debts. I ain't larned 'em to do that. I ain't got much larnin' myself but I do know right from wrong atter I see through a thing."

Professor Herbert went home. Pa and I stayed and swept one hour. It looked funny to see Pa use a broom. He never used one at home. Mom used the broom. Pa used the plow. Pa did hard work. Pa says: "I can't sweep. Durned if I can. Look at th' streaks o' dirt I leave on th' floor! Seems like no work a-tall fer me. Brooms is too light 'r somethin'. I'll jist do th' best I can, Dave. I've been wrong about th' school."

I says: "Did you know Professor Herbert can get a warrant out for you for bringing your pistol to school and showing it in his office! They can railroad you for that!"

"That's all made right," says Pa. "I've made that right. Professor Herbert ain't goin' to take it to court. He likes me. I like 'im. We jist had to get together. He had the remedies. He showed me. You must go on to school. I am as strong a man as ever come out'n th' hills fer my years and th' hard work I've done. But I'm behind, Dave. I'm a little man. Your hands will be softer than mine. Your clothes will be better. You'll allus look cleaner than your old Pap. Jist remember, Dave, to pay your debts and be honest. Jist be kind to animals and don't bother th' snakes. That's all I got agin th' school. Puttin' black snakes to sleep and cuttin' 'em open."

It was late when we got home. Stars were in the sky. The moon was up. The ground was frozen. Pa took his time going home. I couldn't run like I did the night before. It was ten o'clock before we got the work finished, our suppers eaten. Pa sat before the fire and told Mom he was going to take her and show her a germ some time. Mom hadn't seen one either. Pa told her about the high school and the fine man Professor Herbert was. He told Mom about the strange school across the hill and how different it was from the school in their day and time.

THE WHITE CIRCLE

by John Bell Clayton

As soon as I saw Anvil squatting up in the tree like some hateful creature that belonged in trees I knew I had to take a beating and I knew the kind of beating it would be. But still I had to let it be that way because this went beyond any matter of courage or shame.

The tree was *mine*. I want no doubt about that. It was a seedling that grew out of the slaty bank beside the dry creek-mark across the road from the house, and the thirteen small apples it had borne that year were the thirteen most beautiful things on this beautiful earth.

The day I was twelve Father took me up to the barn to look at the colts—Saturn, Jupiter, Devil, and Moonkissed, the whiteface. Father took a cigar out of his vest pocket and put one foot on the bottom plank of the fence and leaned both elbows on the top of the fence and his face looked quiet and pleased and proud and I liked the way he looked because it was as if he had a little joke or surprise that would turn out nice for me.

"Tucker," Father said presently, "I am not unaware of the momentousness of this day. Now there are four of the finest colts in Augusta County; if there are four any finer anywhere in Virginia I don't know where you'd find them unless Arthur Hancock over in Albemarle would have them." Father took one elbow off the fence and looked at me. "Now do you suppose," he asked, in that fine, free, good humor, "that if I were to offer you a little token to commemorate this occasion you could make a choice?"

"Yes sir," I said.

"Which one?" Father asked. "Devil? He's wild."

"No sir," I said. "I would like to have the apple tree below the gate."

Father looked at me for at least a minute. You would have to understand his pride in his colts to understand the way he looked. But at twelve how could I express how *I* felt? My setting such store in having the tree as my own had something to do with the coloring of the apples as they hung among the green leaves; it had something also to do with their ripening, not in autumn when the world was full of apples, but in midsummer when you *wanted* them; but it had more to do with a way of life that had come down through the generations. I would have given one of the apples to Janie. I would have made of it a ceremony. While I would not have said the words, because at twelve you have no such words, I would have handed over the apple with something like this in mind: "Janie, I want to give you this apple. It came from my tree. The tree stands on my father's land. Before my father had the land it belonged to his father, and before that it belonged to my great-grandfather. It's the English family land. It's almost sacred. My possession of this tree forges of me a link in this owning ancestry that must go back clear beyond Moses and all the old Bible folks."

Father looked at me for that slow, peculiar minute in our lives. "All right, son," he said. "The tree is yours in fee simple to bargain, sell, and convey or to keep and nurture and eventually hand down to your heirs or assigns forever unto eternity. You have a touch of poetry in your soul and that fierce, proud love of the land in your heart; when you grow up I hope you don't drink too much."

I didn't know what he meant by that but the tree was mine and now there perched Anvil, callously munching one of my thirteen apples and stowing the rest inside his ragged shirt until it bulged out in ugly lumps. I knew the apples pressed cold against his hateful belly and to me the coldness was a sickening evil.

I picked a rock up out of the dust of the road and tore across the creek bed and said, "All right, Anvil—climb down!"

Anvil's milky eyes batted at me under the strangely fair eyebrows. There was not much expression on his face. "Yaannh!" he said. "You stuck-up little priss, you hit me with that rock. You just do!"

"Anvil," I said again, "climb down. They're my apples."

Anvil quit munching for a minute and grinned at me. "You want an apple? I'll give you one. Yaannh!" He suddenly cocked back his right arm and cracked me on the temple with the half-eaten apple.

I let go with the rock and it hit a limb with a dull chub sound and Anvil said, "You're fixin' to git it—you're real-ly fixin' to git it."

"I'll shake you down," I said. "I'll shake you clear down."

"Clear down?" Anvil chortled. "Where do you think I'm at? Up on top of Walker Mountain? It wouldn't hurt none if I was to fall out of this runty bush on my head."

I grabbed one of his bare feet and pulled backwards, and down Anvil came amidst a flutter of broken twigs and leaves. We both hit the ground. I hopped up and Anvil arose with a faintly vexed expression.

He hooked a leg in back of my knees and shoved a paw against my chin. I went down in the slate. He got down and pinioned my arms with his knees. I tried to kick him in the back of the head but could only flail my feet helplessly in the air.

"You might as well quit kickin'," he said.

He took one of my apples from his shirt and began eating it, almost absent-mindedly.

"You dirty filthy stinkin' sow," I said.

He snorted. "I couldn't be a sow, but you take that back."

"I wish you were fryin' in the middle of hell right this minute."

"Take back the stinkin' part," Anvil said thoughtfully. "I don't stink."

He pressed his knees down harder, pinching and squeezing the flesh of my arms.

I sobbed, "I take back the stinkin' part."

"That's better," Anvil said.

He ran a finger back into his jaw to dislodge a fragment of apple from his teeth. For a moment he examined the fragment and then wiped it on my cheek.

"I'm goin' to tell Father," I said desperately.

"'Father,'" Anvil said with falsetto mimicry. "'Father.' Say 'Old Man.' You think your old man is some stuff on a stick, don't you? You think he don't walk on the ground, don't you? You think you and your whole stuck-up family don't walk on the ground. Say 'Old Man.'"

"Go to hell!"

"Shut up your blubberin'. Say 'Old Man.'"

"Old Man. I wish you were dead."

"Yaannh!" Anvil said. "Stop blubberin'. Now call me 'Uncle Anvil.' Say 'Uncle Sweetie Peetie Tweetie Beg-Your-Pardon Uncle Anvil.' Say it!"

"Uncle Sweetie . . . Uncle Peetie, Tweetie Son-of-a-bitch Anvil."

He caught my hair in his hands and wallowed my head against the ground until I said every bitter word of it. Three times.

Anvil tossed away a spent, maltreated core that had been my apple. He gave my head one final thump upon the ground and said "Yaannh!" again in a satisfied way.

He released me and got up. I lay there with my face muscles twitching in outrage.

Anvil looked down at me. "Stop blubberin'," he commanded.

"I'm not cryin'," I said.

I was lying there with a towering, homicidal detestation, planning to kill Anvil—and the thought of it had a sweetness like summer fruit.

There were times when I had no desire to kill Anvil. I remember the day his father showed up at the school. He was a dirty, half-crazy, itinerant knickknack peddler. He had a club and he told the principal he was going to beat the meanness out of Anvil or beat him to death. Anvil scudded under a desk and lay there trembling and whimpering until the principal finally drove the ragged old man away. I had no hatred for Anvil then.

But another day, just for the sheer filthy meanness of it, he crawled through a classroom window after school hours and befouled the floor. And the number of times he pushed over smaller boys, just to see them hit the packed hard earth of the schoolyard and to watch the fright on their faces as they ran away, was more than I could count.

And still another day he walked up to me as I leaned against the warmth of the schoolhack shed in the sunlight, feeling the nice warmth of the weather-beaten boards.

"They hate me," he said dismally. "They hate me because my old man's crazy."

As I looked at Anvil I felt that in the background I was seeing that demented, bitter father trudging his lonely, vicious way through the world.

"They don't hate you," I lied. "Anyway I don't hate you." That was true. At that moment I didn't hate him. "How about comin' home and stayin' all night with me?"

So after school Anvil went along with me—and threw rocks at me all the way home.

Now I had for him no soft feeling of any kind. I planned —practically—his extinction as he stood there before me commanding me to cease the blubbering out of my heart.

"Shut up now," Anvil said. "I never hurt you. Stop blubberin'."

"I'm not cryin'," I said.

"You're still mad though." He looked at me appraisingly.

"No, I'm not," I lied. "I'm not even mad. I was a little bit mad, but not now."

"Well, whattaya look so funny around the mouth and eyes for?"

"I don't know. Let's go up to the barn and play."

"Play whut?" Anvil looked at me truculently. He didn't know whether to be suspicious or flattered. "I'm gettin' too big to play. To play much, anyway," he added undecidedly. "I might play a little bit if it ain't some sissy game."

"We'll play anything," I said eagerly.

"All right," he said. "Race you to the barn. You start."

I started running toward the wire fence and at the third step he stuck his foot between my legs and I fell forward on my face.

"Yaannh!" he croaked. "That'll learn you."

"Learn me what?" I asked as I got up. "Learn me what?" It seemed important to know that. Maybe it would make some difference in what I planned to do to Anvil. It seemed very important to know what it was that Anvil wanted to, and never could, teach me and the world.

"It'll just learn you," he said doggedly. "Go ahead, I won't trip you any more."

So we climbed the wire fence and raced across the burned field the hogs ranged in.

We squeezed through the heavy sliding doors onto the barn floor, and the first thing that caught Anvil's eye was the irregular circle that father had painted there. He wanted to know what it was and I said "Nothing" because I wasn't yet quite ready, and Anvil forgot about it for the moment and wanted to play jumping from the barn floor out to the top of the fresh rick of golden straw.

I said, "No. Who wants to do that, anyway?"

"I do," said Anvil. "Jump, you puke. Go ahead and jump!"

I didn't want to jump. The barn had been built on a hill. In front the ground came up level with the barn floor, but in back the floor was even with the top of the straw rick, with four wide, terrible yawning feet between.

I said, "Nawh, there's nothin' to jumpin'."

"Oh, there ain't, hanh!" said Anvil. "Well, try it—"

He gave me a shove and I went out into terrifying space. He leaped after and upon me and we hit the pillowy side of the straw rick and tumbled to the ground in a smothering slide.

"That's no fun," I said, getting up and brushing the chaff from my face and hair.

Anvil himself had lost interest in it by now and was idly munching another of my apples.

"I know somethin'," I said. "I know a good game. Come on, I'll show you."

Anvil stung me on the leg with the apple as I raced through the door of the cutting room. When we reached the barn floor his eyes again fell on the peculiar white circle. "That's to play prisoner's base with," I said. "That's the base."

"That's a funny-lookin' base," he said suspiciously. "I never saw any base that looked like that."

I could feel my muscles tensing, but I wasn't particularly excited. I didn't trust myself to look up toward the roof where the big mechanical hayfork hung suspended from the long metal track that ran back over the steaming mows of alfalfa and red clover. The fork had vicious sharp prongs that had never descended to the floor except on one occasion Anvil knew nothing about.

I think Father had been drinking the day he bought the hayfork in Staunton. It was an unwieldy involved contraption of ropes, triggers, and pulleys which took four men to operate. A man came out to install the fork and for several days he climbed up and down ladders, bolting the track in place and arranging the various gadgets. Finally, when he said it was ready, Father had a load of hay pulled into the barn and called the men in from the fields to watch and assist in the demonstration.

I don't remember the details. I just remember that something went very badly wrong. The fork suddenly plunged down with a peculiar ripping noise and embedded itself in the back of one of the work horses. Father said very little. He simply painted the big white circle on the barn floor, had the fork hauled back up to the top, and fastened the trigger around the rung of a stationary ladder eight feet off the floor, where no one could inadvertently pull it.

Then he said quietly, "I don't ever want anyone ever to touch this trip rope or to have occasion to step inside this circle."

So that was why I didn't now look up toward the fork.

"I don't want to play no sissy prisoner's base," Anvil

said. "Let's find a nest of young pigeons."

"All right," I lied. "I know where there's a nest. But one game of prisoner's base first."

"You don't know where there's any pigeon nest," Anvil said. "You wouldn't have the nerve to throw them up against the barn if you did."

"Yes, I would too," I protested. "Now let's play one game of prisoner's base. Get in the circle and shut your eyes and start countin'."

"Oh, all right," Anvil agreed wearily. "Let's get it over with and find the pigeons. Ten, ten, double ten, forty-five—"

"Right in the middle of the circle," I told him. "And count slow. How'm I goin' to hide if you count that way?"

Anvil now counted more slowly. "Five, ten, fifteen—"

I gave Anvil one last vindictive look and sprang up the stationary ladder and swung out on the trip rope of the unpredictable hayfork with all my puny might.

The fork's whizzing descent was accompanied by that peculiar ripping noise. Anvil must have jumped instinctively. The fork missed him by several feet.

For a moment Anvil stood absolutely still. He turned around and saw the fork, still shimmering from its impact with the floor. His face became exactly the pale green of the carbide we burned in our acetylene lighting plant at the house. Then he looked at me, at the expression on my face, and his Adam's apple bobbed queerly up and down, and a little stream of water trickled down his right trouser leg and over his bare foot.

"You tried to kill me," he said thickly.

He did not come toward me. Instead, he sat down. He shook his head sickly. After a few sullen, bewildered moments he reached into his shirt and began hauling out my apples one by one.

"You can have your stinkin' old apples," he said. "You'd do that for a few dried-up little apples. Your old man owns everything in sight. I ain't got nothin'. Go ahead and keep your stinkin' old apples."

He got to his feet and slowly walked out of the door.

Since swinging off the trip rope I had neither moved nor spoken. For a moment more I stood motionless and voiceless and then I ran over and grabbed up the nine apples that were left and called, "Anvil! Anvil!" He continued across the field without even pausing.

I yelled, "Anvil! Wait, I'll give them to you."

Anvil climbed the fence without looking back and set off down the road toward the store. Every few steps he kicked his wet trouser leg.

Three sparrows flew out of the door in a dusty, chattering spiral. Then there was only the image of the hay-fork shimmering and terrible in the great and growing and accusing silence and emptiness of the barn.

THE WISHING WELL

by Phillip Bonosky

BEEZIE WENT HOME that night after listening to the caddy and lay awake thinking of the bottom of the well building higher and higher with dimes, nickels, quarters and half dollars. That had been going on for years, the caddy had guessed; for years—the guys would throw the money into the water, and the girls would, and they'd "wish" —you-know-what-for, said the caddy. Then the girls would go down into the woods with the boys; but Beezie didn't care about that.

"Will you come with me?" he said to Kozik. "Will you come? Just watch, I'll go down. But will you come?"

"If they catch us?"

"Kick us in the ass and let us go. We're just kids," he explained.

"How can we get in?"

"I'll find a way, but will you come?"

Kozik's yellow eyes considered. Over them his lids fell and opened like the lazy wings of a moth.

"How much will you give me?"

"A third," Beezie said.

"No, a half."

"You'll just watch. *I'll* go down the well!"

Kozik stared away.

"How much you think is down there?"

"A hundred dollars!"

"Gee!" His lids opened wide. "A hundred dollars!" he echoed. "You're crazy! Who'd let all that money lay down that old well? *Somebody* would take it! You're crazy!"

"You don't *know!*" Beezie replied. "You don't know *them!* They're rich!"

They pooled their money and took two streetcars—the first one carried them out of town; the second one, ten miles into the country, through the little hamlets, until up on a green hill, like a pearl, sat the big white house, partly screened by elm trees. It was late afternoon and they were hungry, but had no money to buy food. They ate sour-grass. They had no money either to ride back home again in case they failed. They hadn't thought about that.

"We'll wait until it gets dark," Beezie said.

"Then the fellas come down," Kozik protested.

"That's why you gotta watch. They'd see us in the daytime."

"How about dogs?"

"Dogs?"

"Yeah, how about dogs?"

But Beezie didn't answer.

They sat on a rock at the point where the driveway divided from the road. They stared solemnly as the bright sport cars loaded with strange women and stranger-looking men drove up. The cars were jagged with tennis rackets, golf clubs, polo sticks—the unrecognizable tools of their living. The women's hair didn't look like hair to the boys; and the hair on the men was odd, too. They wore sun glasses—tortoise shelled or pink coral, in every shape. They also spoke differently, and though the boys heard whole phrases they understood nothing that was said.

They watched them like exotic birds from a green jungle.

"Besides," Beezie said, remembering the final proof, "it was in the papers—about their doing it; the wishing well, throwing money in it."

"How you going to find where it is?"

"Down there," Beezie said mysteriously, pointing to a clump of trees down the hill from the house. "Down there. That's where."

They were both hungry but didn't realize it. Their hunger was trapped inside their excitement. They lay beside the road, munching sour-grass or chewing orchard grass; they picked off the green haws from the bushes and threw them at ants and at birds. Cars came and went, and each time one arrived both fell silent and stared at its strange cargo.

"Suppose they catch us?" Kozik echoed.

It was still less than dark when, worn out with waiting, Beezie cried: "Let's start!"

"They'll see us!"

"No," he fired back. "Hear the music!"

They stood to listen. From the house on the hill came music. Lights had begun to shine, too. But the music, most of all, came; it made the house seem like a handful of another world set down on top of the hill in the middle of the woods and fields, being by itself.

"They're listening to that. They won't hear us."

There was a wire fence running along the road. It was tipped with sharpened, turned-over naked ends. When they touched it with their hands they jumped back.

"Oh!" Kozik cried, backing away from it and staring at it with horror. His lids fell heavily and then opened.

From behind the charged fence the music came. Beezie's hands tingled and his scalp had grown cold. It seemed to him for a moment that they had taken the wrong streetcar and this was the wrong place, it wasn't even in the same country.

Away from them the fence crossed a creek, and between the creek and the bottom of the fence was a foot and a half of space. They stood above it debating silently for a long time before taking the risk of climbing under the fence. But they only wet their shoes.

Inside the fence it felt different. Now even the music seemed nearer and clearer. Beezie felt his heart pounding right under his shirt; he wanted to still it with his hand.

They followed the creek because this would lead them to it; and as they crawled along, suddenly they heard the patter of horses' hoofs and both sank like shadows into the grass behind the bushes. Sunk there, they saw a man and a girl get off; saw the man take the girl and kiss her.

Lying flat on the ground, suddenly rigid, they watched the man and girl, saw what they did. Kozik pushed his cheeks in with the knuckles of both hands. They burned on his knuckles; his body was straight as a stick against the earth. His teeth began to chatter. Beezie's own mouth was dry as if he had been sucking a stone. His eyes could not close, they burned until tears came, then stung as if filled with sand.

Long after the two had gone, they lay still. They could not get up. Putting his crossed arms before him, Beezie laid his hot forehead on them and closed his eyes. The thick musk of decayed leaves rose and filled his nostrils. There was a glaze of whirling circles in his head. His heart slowly began to fade. He felt himself stretched along and into the ground as he had clutched it and dug into it. He tried to speak through his tiny mouth, but could bring nothing out. He did not look at his friend. He only heard the stubborn chatter of teeth, which slowly died down. He felt Kozik jerk like a dying fish.

Finally, Kozik cried: "Beezie, take me home with you!"

After a minute, he pulled himself up and helped bring Kozik to his feet. He could see his pale face, touched his hand and felt that it was cold and wet and shaking.

They followed the creek on, and when they heard horses again, Kozik shuddered and felt Beezie's hand tighten in his own as he held it to guide him through the dark. Beezie felt that Kozik had forgotten why they had come; he himself had forgotten it. He did not know where they had come to. It was like a fairyland, a strange one, a fearful one. He wanted to turn back with that, big in his head, and take it home, and go immediately to bed, away from every one, and think and think about it. It seemed to him that the fence they had passed under had been mysterious, filled with magic.

To Kozik he said: "Don't forget! Don't forget!"

The music, which somehow had disappeared, now suddenly charged on them. They could distinguish a cymbal clash; even, for one brief moment that made them stand still with cold, the crystal laugh of a girl; then it was shut off.

The creek led through thicker and thicker bushes. Beezie could smell crushed blackberries. A bridle-path followed along but they did not dare to walk the path; instead they threaded themselves through the bushes. When they arrived, at first they didn't recognize the spot. The well was under a pergola, over which grapes grew. There were stone seats around, off a little; inside the pergola was the stone well. It had an old wooden handle, an old green-mossy axle around which the rope wound which let down a wooden bucket into the well. A wooden lid with a hand-carved handle stood beside it, green with faint moss.

Kozik's moth-lids blinked. "How deep is it?" he asked.

Beezie looked at the well, then leaned over into it. He threw a pebble down and listened. A *plunk* followed, and he said, thoughtfully, "It's pretty far down, but not *deep*, I think."

He stood silent. Neither did Kozik speak. Fireflies suddenly swarmed out of the bushes and flew in and out. The music was faint again, but through the trees they could see the lighted windows; then the music, flung at them suddenly, crashed through and jarred him.

"Well," Beezie said, remotely. "I'll go down. You unwind it, slow."

"All right."

"And watch."

"All right."

"When I'm down, you put in the peg in there." He showed how to peg the winder so that it would no longer turn.

He took off his shoes and stockings and rolled up his trouser legs above his knees. The moonlight made his legs look pale. He climbed into the bucket. His white face hovered over the rim of the well for a moment and, hushed, he said: "We'll be rich, Kozik!"

"We'll count it when we get home," Kozik said.

"Yes," Beezie answered. Kozik began to unwind. His white face staring at him, Beezie disappeared.

The wood creaked loud in the stillness. It unwound slowly, and the bucket bumped solemnly from side to side of the well. Looking up, he could see only gray, and with an upward leap of his heart, a single shining star. Kozik he could not see.

If the rope broke, he thought; but he gripped it and felt its strength. Suddenly the unwinding stopped and he dangled in the middle of the well. Looking up he saw silhouettes. Then heard voices. Suddenly money began to fall past him, plunking into the water; there was laughter upstairs. "I was right," he whispered to himself.

He sat twirling slowly, lazily, round and round. As he came near the wall of the well, he gently kicked it and swung away. The wall was slimy and cold to the touch of his bare toes; the well smelled of moss and frogs and salamanders.

Then the rope began to unwind again, its creaking sounding wooden and old, like an ungreased wheel. Abruptly he landed on the water and cried out: "Down!" and the creaking stopped. Kozik leaned his head over and cried: "Down?"

"Down," he answered.

He dangled his feet over into the water and began to reach through it for footing. The water was so cold he gasped. He hunted with his foot but found nothing to stand on. "Jesus," he said to himself.

Now he took his trousers off and let himself over the rim of the bucket into the water, shuddering as he sank, and hanging on to the bucket stretched his feet as far as they could go. Still there was no footing. Now, closing his eyes, he let go of the bucket and sank down over his head. Touching bottom, he fell to his knees and began to grope along the pebbled bottom picking up coins. Then he shot to the water top and his lungs beating, and his teeth beginning to chatter slightly, he dumped the coins into the bucket. Again he let go of it and sank to the bottom; underneath he worked furiously, with slow motions, as in a dream, holding his breath until his head blew up with blood, then he burst to the surface again, and again dumped the coins into the wooden bucket. And again he sank down.

He seemed to rise out of the water like an icicle. His teeth were clenched in his frozen mouth. It was too dark to see what coins he had brought up; his head was so filled with cold he could not hear what Kozik shouted down to him. He heard a cry, but dived down again to the bottom of the well, scratched desperately, then both fists clutched with coins, rose again to the surface.

He reached for the bucket—treaded water reaching for it, his eyes still closed. Then, looking up suddenly, he saw it whirling slowly upward, and beyond it, over the rim of the well, the white face of a girl looking down.

Treading water, he only watched it, unable to think. His head was growing cold from the inside. His feet seemed to tread as if forgotten by him. Then he heard them.

"Look at that!" the man cried. "Money!"

"Oh," the girl said.

"It must have fallen into the bucket instead," the man said.

"This is our lucky night!" the girl cried, laughing.

"Throw it back in," the man ordered.

"No," she said. "If we were smart enough to bring the bucket up—we *win!*" she cried.

"Some of it, anyhow," the man said.

Money spattered down beside him, hitting him, falling around him.

He suddenly began to sink. Loosening one of his fists spasmodically and letting the coins sink, he flung a hand toward the wall and there caught on to a crack filled with moss. Holding on to it, he rested. He smelled worms in the well.

Now the cold grew in his body; he felt it touch his ~es, get into his stomach, encase his lungs with a film of ice. Like a sound over mountains, he felt the first pangs of cramps gathering in his loins, begin slightly to clutch at his stomach. "Let them go away," he said.

In his other fist the coins felt jagged. His hand was shut so tightly over them it seemed to be locked. Trying to open it slightly, he discovered that he could not. He laughed at it, surprised, at his fist.

Above him they were still talking; no longer arguing, they were talking to each other. Where was Kozik? *Where are you, Kozik?* he cried. Did he run home, did he get scared and run home? *No money for you, Kozik,* he cried; *no money for you, you lost your share for running away! You're yellow; you won't get any at all. I'll keep it; I'll learn you to be yellow, Kozik,* he cried. *You'd better come back!*

He felt that his fingers holding the crack were losing sensation. Now, remotely, he felt his legs again. They were still treading, had been treading all the time. He felt grateful to them that they were still treading, because at this point he felt that they didn't need to if they didn't want to. Parts of his body became objectified: his fist was one, his legs were another, his free hand holding to the crack was another, his stomach was another; *himself* was in his head. He promised the parts things and chided them, too; he also reasoned with them. "Hold on tighter," he admonished his hand. To his fist he said: "You hurt."

The water was up to his neck. He had left his shirt on and it was soaked. Suddenly he thought of his pants. Did they throw them away? He cried, "My pants!" He was cold now, it would be cold, how could he go anywhere without pants? He wanted to laugh thinking of himself going home without pants; then his father whipping him— he wanted to cry now; then suddenly his body began to ache from head to foot. His head began to give in; it began to grow colder and colder and throb, it began to collect cold behind his eyes, at the back of his nose. All over it began to attack at once, and he saw himself shutting his eyes and slipping swiftly to the bottom of the well.

"Oh, Kozik!" he cried. "Kozik!"

He lifted his head to stare at the top of the well. The open circle of the well was gone. He couldn't see the star! They had put the lid over him! He was dead. I'm in my grave without a coffin, he said.

Suddenly he began to scream, pulling himself out of the water and falling back again. His feet thrashed beneath him as he screamed. His free hand searched the entire slimy wall for a place to put his feet.

Then he heard the clunk of the bucket against the side of the well. He saw a rim of light, a nimbus, around the bucket, then he caught a glimpse of the star again. It was the bucket coming down. Suddenly he began to sob for it. *Come down, come down,* he cried. *Oh, come down, come down!*

It hit beside him, tilting in the water. It was too far away to reach with his fist, the fist was clenched shut, it could not open. The coins were jagged inside. He let go of the crack with his other hand and fell forward into the water, catching the bucket. It swung toward him and hit his nose, bringing cold tears. He pulled his arm over it, pulled himself half over on it, and lay still. In his mouth he felt the loud chatter of his teeth; they went so fast they began to hurt.

Now, slowly, the bucket began to rise. He lay half across it, his legs dangling, his head pointed downward, his eyes closed. He felt the thick rope throb against his neck. Then he was there; he felt hands, heard a voice.

Kozik struggled with him, finally pulled him off the bucket and fell to the ground with him. He was crying, "Beezie, what's the matter, Beezie? Can't you talk, Beezie? They didn't go away! They kept talking and talking, Beezie, and kissing—they wouldn't go away! They kept kissing, Beezie!"

He looked down; he stared into the blue face of his friend and cried: "Beezie, God, Beezie! You look sick! What's the matter, Beezie, can't you talk?"

Beezie rolled over face down onto the grass. He gripped ⸻th into the grass and bit. His shoulders began to shake. The other started at him with horror and fear. "Beezie!" he kept crying. "It's not my fault, Beezie! It's not my fault! I didn't say to come out here!" Then, suddenly, freshly: "They threw your pants away and I saved them!"

Bit by bit the quaking died down; he felt his separate feet and hands and stomach come together again. The ache subsided behind his eyes, the pain slowly dwindled.

The first thing he said: "Did you get the pants, you said?"

"Yes," the other replied, holding them up. "They're not even wet!"

Beezie stood up and put his trousers on. His fist was still closed. "Let's go home," he said.

They began to walk through the woods; suddenly they began to run. When they came to the fence they crawled under it, drenching themselves; and on the other side they kept running until they reached the car stop.

Beezie stretched his fist over to Kozik.

"Open it," he ordered.

Finger by finger Kozik pulled the paralyzed fingers apart and unfolded the fist. In it lay four dimes and two quarters. They both stared at it for a long time.

Slowly Beezie took one of the quarters and gave it to Kozik.

"This is your share," he said.

The other looked at the quarter. Then, taking a dime, Beezie said, "This is because you didn't run away." He gave it to him.

As they waited for the car to take them home, Kozik asked: "Shall we come back again?"

Beezie thought a long time before he finally answered. "No," he said.

THE FINISH OF PATSY BARNES

by Paul Laurence Dunbar

HIS NAME was Patsy Barnes, and he was a denizen of Little Africa. In fact, he lived on Douglass Street. By all the laws governing the relations between people and their names, he should have been Irish—but he was not. He was colored, and very much so. That was the reason he lived on Douglass Street. The Negro has very strong within him the instinct of colonization and it was in accordance with this that Patsy's mother had found her way to Little Africa when she had come North from Kentucky.

Patsy was incorrigible. Even into the confines of Little Africa had penetrated the truant officer and the terrible penalty of the compulsory education law. Time and time again had poor Eliza Barnes been brought up on account of the shortcomings of that son of hers. She was a hard-working, honest woman, and day by day bent over her tub, scrubbing away to keep Patsy in shoes and jackets, that would wear out so much faster than they could be bought. But she never murmured, for she loved the boy with a deep affection, though his misdeeds were a sore thorn in her side.

She wanted him to go to school. She wanted him to learn. She had the notion that he might become something better, something higher than she had been. But for him school had no charms; his school was the cool stalls in the big livery stable near at hand; the arena of his pursuits its sawdust floor; the height of his ambition, to be a horseman. Either here or in the racing stables at the Fair-grounds he ~~s~~ent his truant hours. It was a school that taught much, ~~P~~atsy was as apt a pupil as he was a constant attendant.

He learned strange things about horses, and fine, sonorous oaths that sounded eerie on his young lips, for he had only turned into his fourteenth year.

A man goes where he is appreciated; then could this slim black boy be blamed for doing the same thing? He was a great favorite with the horsemen, and picked up many a dime or nickel for dancing or singing, or even a quarter for warming up a horse for its owner. He was not to be blamed for this, for, first of all, he was born in Kentucky, and had spent the very days of his infancy about the paddocks near Lexington, where his father had sacrificed his life on account of his love for horses. The little fellow had shed no tears when he looked at his father's bleeding body, bruised and broken by the fiery young two-year-old he was trying to subdue. Patsy did not sob or whimper, though his heart ached, for over all the feeling of his grief was a mad, burning desire to ride that horse.

His tears were shed, however, when, actuated by the idea that times would be easier up North, they moved to Dalesford. Then, when he learned that he must leave his old friends, the horses and their masters, whom he had known, he wept. The comparatively meagre appointments of the Fair-grounds at Dalesford proved a poor compensation for all these. For the first few weeks Patsy had dreams of running away—back to Kentucky and the horses and stables. Then after a while he settled himself with heroic resolution to make the best of what he had, and with a mighty effort took up the burden of life away from his beloved home.

Eliza Barnes, older and more experienced though she was, took up her burden with a less cheerful philosophy than her son. She worked hard, and made a scanty livelihood, it is true, but she did not make the best of what she had. Her complainings were loud in the land, and her wailings for her old home smote the ears of any who would listen to her.

They had been living in Dalesford for a year nearly, when hard work and exposure brought the woman down to bed with pneumonia. They were very poor—too poor even to call in a doctor, so there was nothing to do but to call in the city physician. Now this medical man had too frequent calls into Little Africa, and he did not like to go there. So he was very gruff when any of its denizens called him, and it was even said that he was careless of his patients.

Patsy's heart bled as he heard the doctor talking to his mother:

"Now, there can't be any foolishness about this," he said. "You've got to stay in bed and not get yourself damp."

"How long you think I got to lay hyeah, doctah?" she asked.

"I'm a doctor, not a fortune-teller," was the reply. "You'll lie there as long as the disease holds you."

"But I can't lay hyeah long, doctah, case I ain't got nuffin' to go on."

"Well, take your choice: the bed or the boneyard."

Eliza began to cry.

"You needn't sniffle," said the doctor; "I don't see what you people want to come up here for anyhow. Why don't you stay down South where you belong? You come up here and you're just a burden and a trouble to the city. The South deals with all of you better, both in poverty and crime." He knew that these people did not understand him, but he wanted an outlet for the heat within him.

There was another angry being in the room, and that was Patsy. His eyes were full of tears that scorched him and would not fall. The memory of many beautiful and appropriate oaths came to him; but he dared not let his mother hear him swear. Oh! to have a stone—to be across the street from that man!

When the physician walked out, Patsy went to the bed, took his mother's hand, and bent over shamefacedly to kiss her. He did not know that with that act the Recording Angel blotted out many a curious damn of his.

The little mark of affection comforted Eliza unspeakably. The mother-feeling overwhelmed her in one burst of tears. Then she dried her eyes and smiled at him.

"Honey," she said; "mammy ain' gwine lay hyeah long. She be all right putty soon."

"Nevah you min'," said Patsy with a choke in his voice. "I can do somep'n', an' we'll have anothah doctah."

"La, listen at de chile; what kin you do?"

"I'm goin' down to McCarthy's stable and see if I kin git some horses to exercise."

A sad look came into Eliza's eyes as she said: "You'd bettah not go, Patsy; dem hosses'll kill you yit, des lak dey did yo' pappy."

But the boy, used to doing pretty much as he pleased, was obdurate, and even while she was talking, put on his ragged jacket and left the room.

Patsy was not wise enough to be diplomatic. He went right to the point with McCarthy, the liveryman.

The big red-faced fellow clapped him until he spun round and round. Then he said, "Ye little devil, ye, I've a mind to knock the whole head off o' ye. Ye want harses to exercise, do ye? Well git on that 'un, an' see what ye kin do with him."

The boy's honest desire to be helpful had tickled the big, generous Irishman's peculiar sense of humor, and from now on, instead of giving Patsy a horse to ride now and then as he had formerly done, he put into his charge all the animals that needed exercise.

It was with a king's pride that Patsy marched home with his first considerable earnings.

They were small yet, and would go for food rather than a doctor, but Eliza was inordinately proud, and it was this pride that gave her strength and the desire of life to carry her through the days approaching the crisis of her disease.

As Patsy saw his mother growing worse, saw her gasping for breath, heard the rattling as she drew in the little air that kept going her clogged lungs, felt the heat of her burning hands, and saw the pitiful appeal in her poor eyes, he became convinced that the city doctor was not helping her. She must have another. But the money?

That afternoon, after his work with McCarthy, found him at the Fair-grounds. The spring races were on, and he thought he might get a job warming up the horse of some independent jockey. He hung around the stables, listening to the talk of men he knew and some he had never seen before. Among the latter was a tall, lanky man, holding forth to a group of men.

"No, suh," he was saying to them generally, "I'm goin' to withdraw my hoss, because thaih ain't nobody to ride him as he ought to be rode. I haven't brought a jockey along with me, so I've got to depend on pick-ups. Now, the talent's set again my hoss, Black Boy, because he's been losin' regular, but that hoss has lost for the want of ridin', that's all."

The crowd looked in at the slim-legged, raw-boned horse, and walked away laughing.

"The fools!" muttered the stranger. "If I could ride myself I'd show 'em!"

Patsy was gazing into the stall at the horse.

"What are you doing thaih?" called the owner to him.

"Look hyeah, mistah," said Patsy, "ain't that a bluegrass hoss?"

"Of co'se it is, an' one o' the fastest that evah grazed."

"I'll ride that hoss, mistah."

"What do you know 'bout ridin'?"

"I used to gin'ally be' roun' Mistah Boone's paddock in Lexington, an'—"

"Aroun' Boone's paddock—what! Look here, little nigger, if you can ride that hoss to a winnin' I'll give you more money than you ever seen before."

"I'll ride him."

Patsy's heart was beating very wildly beneath his jacket. That horse. He knew that glossy coat. He knew that raw-boned frame and those flashing nostrils. That black horse there owed something to the orphan he had made.

The horse was to ride in the race before the last. Somehow out of odds and ends, his owner scraped together a suit and colors for Patsy. The colors were maroon and green, a curious combination. But then it was a curious horse, a curious rider, and a more curious combination that brought the two together.

Long before the time for the race Patsy went into the stall to become better acquainted with his horse. The animal turned its wild eyes upon him and neighed. He patted the long, slender head, and grinned as the horse stepped aside as gently as a lady.

"He sholy is full o' ginger," he said to the owner, whose name he had found to be Brackett.

"He'll show 'em a thing or two," laughed Brackett.

"His dam was a fast one," said Patsy, unconsciously.

Brackett whirled on him in a flash. "What do you know about his dam?" he asked.

The boy would have retracted, but it was too late. Stammeringly he told the story of his father's death and the horse's connection therewith.

"Well," said Bracket, "if you don't turn out a hoodoo, you're a winner, sure. But I'll be blessed if this don't sound like a story! But I've heard that story before. The man I got Black Boy from, no matter how I got him, you're too young to understand the ins and outs of poker, told it to me."

When the bell sounded and Patsy went out to warm up, he felt as if he were riding on air. Some of the jockeys laughed at his get-up, but there was something in him—or under him, maybe—that made him scorn their derision. He saw a sea of faces about him, then saw no more. Only a shining white track loomed ahead of him, and a restless steed was cantering with him around the curve. Then the bell called him back to the stand.

They did not get away at first, and back they trooped. A second trial was a failure. But at the third they were off in a line as straight as a chalk-mark. There were Essex and Firefly, Queen Bess and Mosquito, galloping away side by side, and Black Boy a neck ahead. Patsy knew the family reputation of his horse for endurance as well as fire, and began riding the race from the first. Black Boy came of blood that would not be passed, and to this his rider trusted. At the eighth the line was hardly broken, but as the quarter was reached Black Boy had forged a length ahead, and Mosquito was at his flank. Then, like a flash,

Essex shot out ahead under whip and spur, his jockey standing straight in the stirrups.

The crowd in the stand screamed; but Patsy smiled as he lay low over his horse's neck. He saw that Essex had made her best spurt. His only fear was for Mosquito, who hugged and hugged his flank. They were nearing the three-quarter post, and he was tightening his grip on the black. Essex fell back; his spurt was over. The whip fell unheeded on his sides. The spurs dug him in vain.

Black Boy's breath touches the leader's ear. They are neck and neck—nose to nose. The black stallion passes him.

Another cheer from the stand, and again Patsy smiles as they turn into the stretch. Mosquito has gained a head. The colored boy flashes one glance at the horse and rider who are so surely gaining upon him, and his lips close in a grim line. They are half-way down the stretch, and Mosquito's head is at the stallion's neck.

For a single moment Patsy thinks of the sick woman at home and what that race will mean to her, and then his knees close against the horse's sides with a firmer dig. The spurs shoot deeper into the steaming flanks. Black Boy shall win; he must win. The horse that has taken away his father shall give him back his mother. The stallion leaps away like a flash, and goes under the wire—a length ahead.

Then the band thundered, and Patsy was off his horse, very warm and very happy, following his mount to the stable. There, a little later, Brackett found him. He rushed to him, and flung his arms around him.

"You little devil," he cried, "you rode like you were kin to that hoss! We've won! We've won!" And he began sticking banknotes at the boy. At first Patsy's eyes bulged, and then he seized the money and got into his clothes.

"Goin' out to spend it?" asked Brackett.

"I'm goin' for a doctah fu' my mother," said Patsy, "she's sick."

"Don't let me lose sight of you."

"Oh, I'll see you again. So long," said the boy.

An hour later he walked into his mother's room with a very big doctor, the greatest the druggist could direct him to. The doctor left his medicines and his orders, but, when Patsy told his story, it was Eliza's pride that started her on the road to recovery. Patsy did not tell his horse's name.

A GOOD LONG SIDEWALK

by William Melvin Kelley

THE BARBERSHOP was warm enough to make Carlyle Bedlow sleepy, and smelled of fragrant shaving soap. A fat man sat in the great chair, his stomach swelling beneath the striped cloth. Standing behind him in a white, hair-linted tunic which buttoned along one shoulder, Garland, the barber, clacked his scissors. Garland's hair was well kept, his sideburns cut off just where his wire eye-glasses passed back to his ears. "Hello, Carlyle. How you doing?" He looked over the tops of his glasses. "So you decided to let me make a living, huh?"

"Yes, sir." Carlyle smiled. He liked Garland.

"Taking advantage of Bronx misery?"

"Sir?"

"I mean when folks is having trouble getting their cars dug out, you making money shoveling Bronx snow."

"Oh. Yes, sir." Garland was always teasing him because Carlyle's family had moved recently from Harlem to this neighborhood in the Bronx. He maintained Carlyle thought the Bronx was full of hicks.

"Okay. You're next. I'll take some of that snow money from you." He returned to the fat man's head.

Carlyle leaned his shovel in the corner, stamped his feet, took off his jacket, sat down in a wire-backed chair and picked up a comic book. He had already read it, and put it down to watch the barber shave the fat man's neck with the electric clippers.

The fat man, who had been talking when Carlyle came in, continued: "Can't see why he'd want to do that, can

you, Garland? But ain't that just like a nigger!" He was
very dark. The skin under his chin was heavily pocked and
scarred.

"And just like a white woman too!"

"Man, these cats marry some colored girl when they
starting out, just singing in joints and dives. She supports
him while he's trying to get ahead. But then he gets a hit
record, or a job at the Waldorf and—bingo!—he drops her
quick, gets a divorce, and marries some white bitch."

"White chicks know where it's at. They laying in wait
for him. When he makes it, they'll cut in on a good thing
every time. Anyway, it won't last a year. And you can
quote me on that." Garland finished cutting great patches
of hair from the man's head and started to shape the back.

A short, light-skinned Negro opened the door and
leaned in. "Hello, Garland." He did not close the door and
cold wind blasted in around him.

"Say, man, how you doing? You after the boy there. All
right?" He continued to work, hardly looking at the head
in front of him; he could cut hair blindfolded.

The short man nodded and closed the door behind him.
He removed his coat, put his gloves carefully into a
pocket, sat down, and stretched. Only then did he take off
his hat. His hair was straight and black; he did not seem
to need a haircut. "I read in *The Amsterdam* how Mister
Cool and his white sweetie finally got shackled."

"Yes, sir. We just talking about that." Garland reached
behind him, touched a switch and from an aluminum box,
lather billowed into his palm. "Ain't that just like a
Negro!"

"And like a white bitch too!" the fat man added. "Don't
trim the sideburns, Garland. Just around the ears. I'll trim
the sideburns myself."

Garland nodded. "Man, I seen the same thing happen a
thousand times. A Negro making more money than a
white man starting to act foolish like a white man. Even
though he should know better. I guess it ain't really that
Negro's fault. All his life he been poor and a nobody."

Garland put the lather behind the fat man's ears. "So as soon as he gets some money it's bound to mess up his mind."

"Don't touch the sideburns, Garland." The fat man shifted under the striped sheet. "Yeah, I think you right. And them white bitches is waiting to ambush him."

The short man folded his thin arms across his chest. "Well, don't all a colored man's problems begin with Mister Charlie and Miss Mary?"

"Mostly when Miss Mary wants to make time with her nigger chauffeur or handyman and Mister Charlie finds out about it. He don't blame Miss Mary for it, that's sure." The fat man leaned forward.

Garland stopped shaving, reflecting. "Mostly when you find some white woman being nice to you, nicer than she ought to be. Then watch out!" He started to shave behind the fat man's ears. "Them white women know where it's at."

The short man nodded. "Yeah, but I can't see why no colored man'd want to marry no white chick on purpose like Mister Cool did. Not when there's so many fine spade chicks around."

Garland agreed. "I like my women the way I like my coffee: hot, strong, and black!"

The fat man jerked his head. "I guess he thinks he taking a step up. Now he thinks he better than all the other boots standing on the corner. He's got himself a white recording contract with a big white company, and a booking at a fine, white night club, and a white Cadillac and an apartment on Park Avenue painted all white and a white bitch too. Why, man, he almost white himself . . . except for one thing: he still a nigger!"

They all laughed, slapping their thighs.

It seemed much colder with his hair cut short, his neck shaved clean. Carlyle trudged flat-footed, planting his feet firmly so as not to slip, up the middle of the carless street, through the shadows cast by the snow-clogged trees. He wished he could go home, take off his wet shoes, listen to records, and read the paper that each night his father carried home tucked under his arm. He knew too that the later it got, the angrier his father would be; his father liked to eat as soon as he came home. Besides, his father would want him or his little brother to clear their own driveway and Carlyle had not asked to take the shovel. He decided then, walking along the rutted street, he would not waste his time with small jobs; he would look for a long snow-banked walk of a house set way back from the street.

This is what he finally found, down a solitary side street lit faintly by a single street lamp at the middle of the block; the house, set back on a short hill that surely, in the spring and summer, would be a thick lawn, perhaps bordered with flowers. Snow clung to the empty, blackened branches of a hedge concealing a grotesque iron fence. The house too was grotesque, painted gray, its gables hung with dagger-like icicles.

He hesitated a moment, looking up at the house; there did not seem to be any light burning, and he did not want to wade twenty or thirty feet through shin-deep snow only to find no one at home. Going farther on up the sidewalk, he found a lighted window down the side near the back and he returned to the gate and started up the drifted walk.

The porch was wood and clunked hollow when he stamped the snow from his feet. He climbed the steps gingerly and peered at the names on the door-bell. If there was a man's name, he still might not find work—women living alone or old couples more usually needed someone to clean snow. There was a woman's name—Elizabeth Reuben—and a man's too, but his, which was typed, had been recently crossed out. Carlyle rang the bell.

No longer walking, his feet got cold very quickly and when, after what seemed a long while, the door opened—and then only a crack—he was hopping from one foot to the other.

"Yes? What is it?" He could see a nose and one eye, could hear a woman's voice.

"Miz Reuben?" He slurred the 'miss' or 'missus' so as not to insult her either way.

"Yes."

"Would you like to have your walk shoveled?" He moved closer and spoke to the nose and eye.

There was a pause while she looked him over, up and down, and inspected the shovel he held in his hand. "No. I'm sorry. I don't think so."

"Well, uh . . ." There was nothing else to say. He thanked her and turned away.

"Wait!" It sounded almost like a scream. And then softer: "Young man, wait."

He turned back and found the door swung wide. The nose and eye had grown to a small, plumpish, white woman of about forty in a pale blue wool dress. She was not exactly what he would have called pretty, but she was by no means a hag. She was just uninteresting looking. Her hair was a dull brown combed into a style that did her no good; her eyes were flat and gray like cardboard. "On second thought, young man, I think it would be nice to have my walk cleaned off. I'm expecting some visitors and it will make it easier for them . . . to find me." She smiled at him. "But come inside; you must be frozen solid walking around in all this snow and cold."

"That's all right, ma'am. I'll start right away." He took a step back and lifted his shovel.

"You do as I say and come in the house this very moment." She was still smiling, but there was enough of a mother's tone in her voice to make him walk past her through the door, which she closed behind him. "Rest your coat and shovel there and follow me. I'm taking you into the kitchen to put something warm into your stomach."

He did as she ordered and walked behind her down the hall, lit by a low-watt bulb in a yellowing shade.

The first thing he noticed was that the kitchen smelled of leaking gas. There was a huge pile of rags and bits of cloth on the table in the center of the room. There were more rags on the window sill and stuffed at the bottom of the back door.

She saw him looking at them. "It's an old house. It gets very drafty." She smiled nervously, wringing her hands. "Now, are you old enough to drink coffee? Or would you rather have hot chocolate?"

He had remained on his feet. She bustled to the table and swept the rags onto the floor with her arm. "Sit down, please." He did. "Now, what would you rather have?"

"Hot chocolate, please."

"Hot chocolate? Good. That's better for you." She headed toward the stove, almost running; it was big and old-fashioned with a shelf for salt and pepper above the burners. "What's your name, dear?"

"Carlyle, ma'am. Carlyle Bedlow."

"Carlyle? Did you know you were named after a famous man?"

"No, ma'am. I was just named after my father. His name's—"

She was laughing, shrilly, unhappily. He had said something funny but did not know what it was. It made him uneasy.

"What, dear? You started to say something. I interrupted you."

"Nothing, ma'am." He was wondering now what he had said, and why she was being so nice, giving him hot chocolate. Maybe she was giving him the hot chocolate so she could talk to him about things he did not understand and laugh at his ignorance. It was just like the men in the barbershop said: Most of a colored man's trouble began with white people. They were always laughing and making fun of Negroes. . . .

"Do you like your hot chocolate sweet, Carlyle? I can put some sugar in it for you." Behind her voice he could hear the milk sizzling around the edges of the saucepan, could hear the gas feeding the flame.

"Yes, ma'am. I like it sweet."

The milk sizzled louder still as she poured it across the hot sides into his cup. She brought it and sat across from him on the edge of her chair, waiting for him to taste it. He did so and found it good; with his mind's eye, he followed it down his throat and into his stomach.

"Is it good?" Her gray eyes darted across his face.

"Yes, ma'am."

She smiled and seemed pleased. That puzzled him. If she had him in to laugh at him, why was she so anxious to get him warm, why did she want him to like the hot chocolate? There had to be some other reason, but just then the chocolate was too good to think about it. He took a big swallow.

"Well now, let's get down to business. I've never had to hire anybody to do this before. I used to do it myself when I was younger and . . . then . . . there was a man here who'd do it for me . . . but he's not here any more." She trailed off, caught herself. "How much do you usually get for a stoop and a walk that long?" She smiled at him again. It was a fleeting smile which warmed only the corners of her mouth and left her eyes sad. "I've been very nice to you. I should think you'd charge me less than usual."

So that was it! She wanted him to do her walk for practically nothing! White people were always trying to cheat Negroes. He had heard his father say that, cursing the Jews in Harlem. He just stared at her, hating her.

She waited an instant for him to answer then started to figure out loud. "Well, let's see. That's a long walk and there's the sidewalk and the stoop and the steps and it's very cold and I probably can't get anyone else . . . It's a question of too little supply and a great deal of demand." She was talking above him again. "I'd say I'd be getting off well if I gave you five dollars." She stopped and looked across at him, helplessly. "Does that sound fair? I really don't know."

He continued to stare, but now because he could hardly believe what she said. At the most, he would have charged only three dollars, and had expected her to offer one.

She filled in the silence. "Yes, five. That sounds right."

He finished his chocolate with a gulp. "But, ma'am, I wouldn't-a charged you but three. Really!"

"Three? That doesn't sound like enough." She bolted from the table and advanced on him. "Well, I'll give you the extra two for being honest. Perhaps you can come back and do something else for me." She swooped on him, hugged, and kissed him. The kiss left a wet, cold spot on his cheek. He lurched away, surprised, knocking the cup and saucer from the table. The saucer broke in two; the cup bounced, rolled, lopsided and crazy, under the table.

"No, ma'am." He jumped to his feet. "I'm sorry, ma'am."

"That's all right. It's all right. I'm sor—That's all right about the saucer." She scrambled to her knees and began to pick up the pieces and the cup. Once she had them in her lap, she sat, staring away at nothing, shaking her head.

Now he knew for certain what she was up to; he remembered what Garland had said: When you find some white woman being nicer than she ought to be, then watch out! She wanted to make time with him. He started from the kitchen. Maybe he could leave before it was too late.

"Wait, young man." She stood up. "I'll pay you now and you won't have to come inside when you're through." She pushed by him and hurried down the shadowy hallway. He followed her as before, but kept his distance.

Her purse was hanging on a peg on the coat-rack, next to his own jacket. She took them both down, handed him his jacket, averting her eyes, and fumbled in her purse, produced a wallet, unzipped it, pulled out a bill and handed it to him.

"But it's a five, ma'am." He could not understand why she wanted to pay him that much now that he was not going to make time with her.

She looked at him for the first time, her eyes wet. "I told you I'd pay you five, didn't I?"

"Yes, ma'am."

"All right. Do a good job. And remember, don't come back."

"Yes, ma'am."

"You let yourself out." She started to the back of the house even before he had finished buttoning his jacket. By the time he opened the door she was far down the hall, and, as he closed it behind him and stepped into the dark, twinkling cold, he could hear her in the kitchen. She was tearing rags.

The next evening the white woman was in the newspaper. A boy trying to deliver a package had found her in the gas-filled kitchen, slumped over a table piled high with rags. Carlyle's father, who saw it first, mentioned it at dinner. "Had a suicide a couple blocks from here." He told who and where.

Carlyle sat staring at his plate.

His father went on: "White folks! Man, if they had to be colored for a day, they'd all kill they-selves. We wouldn't have no race problem then. White folks don't know what hard life is. What's wrong, Junior?"

"She was a nice lady."

His parents and his little brother looked at him.

"You know her, Junior?" His mother put down her fork.

"She was a nice lady, Mama. I shoveled her walk yesterday. She gave me five dollars."

"Oh, Junior." His mother sighed.

"Five dollars?" His father leaned forward. "Crazy, huh?"

"Have some respect!" His mother turned on his father angrily.

Carlyle looked at his mother. "Are white people all bad? There's some good ones, ain't there, Mama?"

"Of course, Junior." His mother smiled. "What made you think—"

"Sure, there is, Junior." His father was smiling too. "The dead ones is good."

PRELUDE

by Albert Halper

I WAS COMING HOME from school, carrying my books by a
strap, when I passed Gavin's poolroom and saw the big
guys hanging around. They were standing in front near the
windows, looking across the street. Gavin's has a kind of
thick window curtain up to eye level, so all I saw was their
heads. The guys were looking at Mrs. Oliver, who lately
has started to get talked about. Standing in her window
across the street, Mrs. Oliver was doing her nails. Her
nice red hair was hanging loose down her back. She
certainly is a nice-looking woman. She comes to my
father's newspaper stand on the corner and buys five or
six movie magazines a week, also the afternoon papers.
Once she felt me under the chin, and laughed. My father
laughed, too, stamping about in his old worn leather
jacket to keep warm. My old man stamps a lot because he
has leg pains and he's always complaining about a heavy
cold in his head.

When I passed the poolroom one or two guys came out.
"Hey, Ike, how's your good-looking sister?" they called, but
I didn't turn around. The guys are eighteen or nineteen and
haven't ever had a job in their life. "What they need is
work," my father is always saying when they bother him
too much. "They're not bad; they get that way because
there's nothing to do," and he tries to explain the meanness
of their ways. But I can't see it like my father. I hate those
fellas and I hope every one of them dies under a truck.
Every time I come home from school past Lake Street
they jab me, and every time my sister Syl comes along they
say things. So when one of them, Fred Gooley, calls, "Hey,

Ike, how's your sister?" I don't answer. Besides, Ike isn't my name anyway. It's Harry.

I passed along the sidewalk, keeping close to the curb. Someone threw half an apple but it went over my head. When I went a little farther someone threw a stone. It hit me in the back of the leg and stung me but it didn't hurt much. I kept a little toward the middle of the sidewalk because I saw a woman coming the other way and I knew they wouldn't throw.

When I reached the corner under the Elevated two big news trucks were standing with their motors going, giving my father the latest editions. The drivers threw the papers onto the sidewalk with a nice easy roll so the papers wouldn't get hurt. The papers are bound with that heavy yellow cord which my father saves and sells to the junkyard when he fills up a bag. "All right, Silverstein," a driver called out. "We'll give you a five-star at six," and both trucks drove off.

The drivers are nice fellas and when they take back the old papers they like to kid my old man. They say, "Hey, you old banker, when are you gonna retire?" or, "Let's roll him, boys, he's got bags of gold in his socks." Of course they know my old man isn't wealthy and that the bags in the inside of the newsstand hold only copper pennies. But they like to kid him and they know he likes it. Sometimes the guys from Gavin's pitch in, but the truck drivers would flatten them if they ever got rough with my old man.

I came up to the newsstand and put my school books inside. "Well, Pa," I said, "you can go to Florida now." So my Pa went to "Florida," that is, a chair near the radiator that Nick Pappas lets him use in his restaurant. He has to use Nick's place because our own flat is too far away, almost a quarter-mile off.

While my father was in Nick's place another truck came to a stop. They dropped off a big load of early sport editions and yelled, "Hey, there, Harry, how's the old man?" I checked off the papers, yelling back, "He's okay, he's in Nick's." Then the truck drove away and the two helpers waved.

I stood around, putting the papers on the stand and making a few sales. The first ten minutes after coming home from school and taking care of the newsstand always excites me. Maybe it's the traffic. The trucks and cars pound along like anything and of course there's the Elevated right up above you which thunders to beat the band. We have our newsstand right up against a big El post and the stand is a kind of cabin which you enter from the side. But we hardly use it, only in the late morning and around two P.M., when business isn't very rushing. Customers like to see you stand outside over the papers ready for business and not hidden inside where they can't get a look at you at all. Besides, you have to poke your head out and stretch your arm to get the pennies, and kids can swipe magazines from the sides, if you don't watch. So we most always stand outside the newsstand, my father, and me, and my sister. Anyhow, I like it. I like everything about selling papers for my father. The fresh air gets me and I like to talk to customers and see the rush when people are let out from work. And the way the news trucks bring all the new editions so we can see the latest headlines, like a bank got held up on the South Side on Sixty-third Street, or the Cubs are winning their tenth straight and have a good chance to cop the pennant, is exciting.

The only thing I don't like is those guys from Gavin's. But since my father went to the police station to complain they don't come around so often. My father went to the station a month ago and said the gang was bothering him, and Mr. Fenway, he's the desk sergeant there, said, "Don't worry any more about it, Mr. Silverstein, we'll take care of it. You're a respectable citizen and taxpayer and you're entitled to protection. We'll take care of it." And the next day they sent over a patrolman who stood around almost two hours. The gang from Gavin's saw him and started to go away, but the cop hollered, "Now listen, don't bother this old fella. If you bother him any I'll have to run some of you in."

And then one of the guys recognized that the cop was Butch, Fred Gooley's cousin. "Listen who's talkin'," he yells back. "Hey, Fred, they got your cousin Butch takin' care of the Yid." They said a lot of other things until the cop got mad and started after them. They ran faster than lightning, separating into alleys. The cop came back empty-handed and said to my father, "It'll blow over, Mr. Silverstein; they won't give you any more trouble." Then he went up the street, turning into Steuben's bar.

Well, all this happened three or four weeks ago and so far the gang has let us alone. They stopped pulling my sixteen-year-old sister by her sweater and when they pass the stand going home to supper all they give us is dirty looks. During the last three or four days, however, they passed by and kinda muttered, calling my father a communist banker and me and my sister reds. My father says they really don't mean it, it's the hard times and bad feelings, and they got to put the blame on somebody, so they put the blame on us. It's certain speeches on the radio and the pieces in some of the papers, my father told us. "Something is happening to some of the people and we got to watch our step," he says.

I am standing there hearing the traffic and thinking it over when my little fat old man comes out from Nick's looking like he liked the warm air in Nick's place. My old man's cheeks looked rosy, but his cheeks are that way from high blood pressure and not from good health. "Well, colonel," he says smiling, "I am back on the job." So we stand around, the two of us, taking care of the trade. I hand out change snappy and say thank you after each sale. My old man starts to stamp around in a little while and, though he says nothing, I know he's got pains in his legs again. I look at the weather forecast in all the papers and some of them say flurries of snow and the rest of them say just snow. "Well, Pa," I tell my old man, "maybe I can go skating tomorrow if it gets cold again."

Then I see my sister coming from high school carrying her briefcase and heading this way. Why the heck doesn't she cross over so she won't have to pass the poolroom, I say to myself; why don't she walk on the other side of the street? But that's not like Sylvia; she's a girl with a hot temper, and when she thinks she is right you can't tell her a thing. I knew she wouldn't cross the street and then cross back, because according to her, why, that's giving in. That's telling those hoodlums that you're afraid of their guts. So she doesn't cross over but walks straight on. When she comes by the pool hall two guys come out and say something to her. She just holds herself tight and goes right on past them both. When she finally comes up she gives me a poke in the side. "Hello, you mickey mouse, what mark did you get in your algebra exam?" I told her I got A, but the truth is I got a C.

"I'll check up on you later," she says to me. "Pa, if he's lying to us we'll fine him ten years!"

My father started to smile and said, "No, Harry is a good boy, two years is enough."

So we stand around kidding and pretty soon, because the wind is coming so sharp up the street, my old man has to "go to Florida" for a while once more. He went into Nick's for some "sunshine," he said, but me and Syl could tell he had the pains again. Anyway, when he was gone we didn't say anything for a while. Then Hartman's furniture factory, which lately has been checking out early, let out and we were busy making sales to the men. They came up the sidewalk, a couple of hundred, all anxious to get home, so we had to work snappy. But Syl is a fast worker, faster than me, and we took care of the rush all right. Then we stood waiting for the next rush from the Hillman's cocoa factory up the block to start.

We were standing around when something hit me in the head, a half of a rotten apple. It hurt a little. I turned quick but didn't see anybody, but Syl started yelling. She was pointing to a big El post across the street behind which a guy was hiding.

"Come on, show your face," my sister was saying. "Come on, you hero, show your yellow face!" But the guy sneaked away, keeping the post between. Syl turned to me and her face was boiling. "The rats! It's not enough with all the trouble over in Europe; they have to start it here."

Just then our old man came out of Nick's and when he

saw Syl's face he asked what was the matter.

"Nothing," she says. "Nothing, I'm just thinking."

But my old man saw the half of a rotten apple on the sidewalk, and at first he didn't say anything but I could see he was worried. "We just have to stand it," he said, like he was speaking to himself, "we just have to stand it. If we give up the newsstand where else can we go?"

"Why do we have to stand it?" I exploded, almost yelling. "Why do we—"

But Mrs. Oliver just then came up to the stand, so I had to wait on her. Besides, she's a good customer and there's more profit on two or three magazines than from a dozen papers.

"I'll have a copy of *Film Fan,* a copy of *Breezy Stories* and a copy of *Movie Stars on Parade,*" she says. I go and reach for the copies.

"Harry is a nice boy," Mrs. Oliver told my father, patting my arm. "I'm very fond of him."

"Yes, he's not bad," my father answered smiling. "Only he has a hot temper once in a while."

But who wouldn't have one, that's what I wanted to say! Who wouldn't? Here we stand around minding our own business and the guys won't let us alone. I tell you sometimes it almost drives me crazy. We don't hurt anybody and we're trying to make a living, but they're always picking on us and won't let us alone. It's been going on for a couple of years now, and though my old man says it'll pass with the hard times, I know he's worried because he doesn't believe what he says. He reads the papers as soon as he gets them from the delivery trucks and lately the news about Europe is all headlines and I can see that it makes him sick. My old man has a soft heart and every time he sees in the papers that something bad in Europe has happened again he seems to grow older and he stands near the papers kind of small and all alone. I tell you, sometimes it almost drives me crazy. My old man should be down in Florida, where he can get healthy, not in Nick Pappas' "Florida," but down in real Florida where you have to go by train. That's where he should be. Then maybe his legs would be all right and he wouldn't have that funny color in his cheeks. Since our mother died last year it seems the doctor's treatments don't make him any better, and he has to skip a treatment once in a while because he says it costs too much. But when he stands there with a customer chuckling you think he's healthy and hasn't got any worries and you feel maybe he has a couple thousand in the bank.

And another thing, what did he mean when he said something two days ago when the fellas from Gavin's passed by and threw a stone at the stand? What did he mean, that's what I want to know. Gooley had a paper rolled up with some headlines about Europe on it and he wiggled it at us and my father looked scared. When they were gone my father said something to me, which I been thinking and thinking about. My Pa said we got to watch our step extra careful now because there's no other place besides this country where we can go. We've always been picked on, he said, but we're up against the last wall now, he told me, and we got to be calm because if they start going after us here there's no other place where we can go. I been thinking and thinking about that, especially the part about the wall. When he said that, his voice sounded funny and I felt like our newsstand was a kind of island and if that went we'd be under the waves.

"Harry, what are you thinking of?" Mrs. Oliver asked me. "Don't I get any change?" She was laughing.

And then I came down from the clouds and found she had given me two quarters. I gave her a nickel change. She laughed again. "When he looks moody and kind of sore like that, Mr. Silverstein, I think he's cute."

My old man crinkled up his eyes and smiled. "Who can say, Mrs. Oliver. He should only grow up to be a nice young man and a good citizen and a credit to his country. That's all I want."

"I'm sure Harry will." Mrs. Oliver answered, then talked to Syl a while and admired Syl's new sweater and was about to go away. But another half of a rotten apple came over and splashed against the stand. Some of it splashed against my old man's coat sleeve. Mrs. Oliver turned around and got mad.

"Now you boys leave Mr. Silverstein alone! You've been pestering him long enough! He's a good American citizen who doesn't hurt anybody! You leave him alone!"

"Yah!" yelled Gooley, who ducked behind an El post with two other guys. "Yah! Sez you!"

"You leave him alone!" hollered Mrs. Oliver.

"Aw, go peddle your papers," Gooley answered. "Go run up a rope."

"Don't pay any attention to them," Syl told Mrs. Oliver. "They think they're heroes, but to most people they're just yellow rats."

I could tell by my old man's eyes that he was nervous and wanted to smooth things over, but Syl didn't give him a chance. When she gets started and knows she's in the right not even the Governor of the State could make her keep quiet.

"Don't pay any attention to them," she said in a cutting voice while my old man looked anxious. "When men hide behind Elevated posts and throw rotten apples at women you know they're not men but just things that wear pants. In Europe they put brown shirts on them and call them saviors of civilization. Here they haven't got the shirts yet and hang around poolrooms."

Every word cut like a knife and the guys ducked away. If I or my father would have said it we would have been nailed with some rotten fruit, but the way Syl has of getting back at those guys makes them feel like yellow dogs. I guess that's why they respect her even though they hate her, and I guess that's why Gooley and one or two of his friends are always trying to get next to her and date her up.

Mrs. Oliver took Syl's side and was about to say something more when Hillman's cocoa factory up the block let out and the men started coming up the street. The 4:45 rush was on and we didn't have time for anything, so Mrs. Oliver left, saying she'd be back when the blue-streak edition of the *News* would arrive. Me and Syl were busy handing out the papers and making change and our Pa helped us while the men took their papers and hurried for the El. It started to get darker and colder and the traffic grew heavier along the street.

Then the *Times* truck, which was a little late, roared up and dropped a load we were waiting for. I cut the strings and stacked the papers and when my father came over and read the first page he suddenly looked scared. In his eyes there was that hunted look I had noticed a couple of days ago. I started to look at the first page of the paper while my old man didn't say a word. Nick came to the window and lit his new neon light and waved to us. Then the light started flashing on and off, flashing on the new headlines. It was all about Austria and how people were fleeing toward the borders and trying to get out of the country before it was too late. My old man grew sick and looked kind of funny and just stood there. Sylvia, who is active in the high-school social science club, began to read the *Times* out loud and started analyzing the news to us; but our Pa didn't need her analysis and kept standing there kind of small with that hunted look on his face. He looked sick all right. It almost drove me crazy.

"For Pete's sake," I yelled at Syl. "Shut up, shut up!"

Then she saw our Pa's face, looked at me, and didn't say anything more.

In a little while it was after five and Syl had to go home and make supper. "I'll be back in an hour," she told me. "Then Pa can go home and rest a bit and me and you can take care of the stand." I said all right.

After she was gone it seemed kind of lonesome. I couldn't stop thinking about what my father had said about this being our last wall. It got me feeling funny and I didn't want to read the papers any more. I stood there feeling queer, like me and my old man were standing on a little island and the waves were coming up. There was still a lot of traffic and a few people came up for papers, but from my old man's face I could tell he felt the same as me.

But pretty soon some more editions began coming and we had to check and stack them up. More men came out from factories on Walnut Street and we were busy making sales. It got colder than ever and my old man began to stamp again. "Go into Nick's, Pa," I told him. "I can handle it out here." But he wouldn't do it because just then another factory let out and we were swamped for a while. "Hi, there, Silverstein," some of the men called to him, "what's the latest news, you king of the press?" They took the papers, kidding him, and hurried up the stairs to the Elevated, reading all about Austria and going home to eat. My father kept staring at the headlines and couldn't take his eyes off the print where it said that soldiers were pouring across the border and mobs were robbing people they hated and spitting on them and making them go down on their hands and knees to scrub the streets. My old man's eyes grew small, like he had the toothache and he shook his head like he was sick. "Pa, go into Nick's," I told him. He just stood there, sick over what he read.

Then the guys from Gavin's poolroom began passing the stand on their way home to supper after a day of just killing time. At first they looked as if they wouldn't bother us. One or two of them said something mean to us, but my old man and me didn't answer. If you don't answer hoodlums, my father once told me, sometimes they let you alone.

But then it started. The guys who passed by came back and one of them said: "Let's have a little fun with the Yids." That's how it began. A couple of them took some magazines from the rack and said they wanted to buy a copy and started reading.

In a flash I realized it was all planned out. My father looked kind of worried but stood quiet. There were about eight or nine of them, all big boys around eighteen and nineteen, and for the first time I got scared. It was just after six o'clock and they had picked a time when the newspaper trucks had delivered the five-star and when all the factories had let out their help and there weren't many people about. Finally one of them smiled at Gooley and said, "Well, this physical culture magazine is mighty instructive, but don't you think we ought to have some of the exercises demonstrated?" Gooley said, "Sure, why not?"

So the first fella pointed to some pictures in the magazine and wanted me to squat on the sidewalk and do the first exercise. I wouldn't do it. My father put his hand on the fella's arm and said, "Please, please." But the guy pushed my father's hand away.

"We're interested in your son, not you. Go on, squat."

"I won't," I told him.

"Go on," he said. "Do the first exercise so that the boys can learn how to keep fit."

"I won't," I said.

"Go on," he said, "do it."

"I won't."

Then he came over to me smiling, but his face looked nasty. "Do it. Do it if you know what's good for you."

"Please, boys," said my Pa. "Please go home and eat and don't make trouble. I don't want to have to call a policeman—"

But before I knew it someone got behind me and tripped me so that I fell on one knee. Then another of them pushed me, trying to make me squat. I shoved someone and then someone hit me, and then I heard someone trying to make them stop. While they held me down on the sidewalk I wiggled and looked up. Mrs. Oliver, who had come for the blue-flash edition, was bawling them out.

"You let him alone! You tramps, you hoodlums, you let him alone!" She came over and tried to help me, but they pushed her away. Then Mrs. Oliver began to yell as two guys twisted my arm and told me to squat.

By this time a few people were passing and Mrs. Oliver called at them to interfere. But the gang were big fellows and there were eight or nine of them, and the people were afraid.

Then while they had me down on the sidewalk Syl came running up the street. When she saw what was happening she began kicking them and yelling and trying to make them let me up. But they didn't pay any attention to her, merely pushing her away.

"Please," my Pa kept saying. "Please let him up; he didn't hurt you. I don't want to have to call the police—"

Then Syl turned to the people who were watching and yelled at them. "Why don't you help us? What are you standing there for?" But none of them moved. Then Syl began to scream:

"Listen, why don't you help us? Why don't you make them stop picking on us? We're human beings the same as you!"

But the people just stood there afraid to do a thing. Then while a few guys held me, Gooley and about four others went for the stand, turning it over and mussing and stamping on all the newspapers they could find. Syl started to scratch them, so they hit her, then I broke away to help her, and then they started socking me too. My father tried to reach me, but three guys kept him away. Four guys got me down and started kicking me and all the time my father was begging them to let me up and Syl was screaming at the people to help. And while I was down, my face was squeezed against some papers on the sidewalk telling about Austria and I guess I went nuts while they kept hitting me, and I kept seeing the headlines against my nose.

Then someone yelled, "Jiggers, the cops!" and they got off of me right away. Nick had looked out the window and had called the station, and the guys let me up and beat it away fast.

But when the cops came it was too late; the stand was a wreck. The newspapers and magazines were all over the sidewalk and the rack that holds the *Argosy* and *Western Aces* was all twisted up. My Pa, who looked sicker than ever, stood there crying and pretty soon I began to bawl. People were standing looking at us like we were some kind of fish, and I just couldn't help it, I started to bawl.

Then the cops came through the crowd and began asking questions right and left. In the end they wanted to take us to the station to enter a complaint, but Syl wouldn't go. She looked at the crowd watching and she said, "What's the use? All those people standing around and none of them would help!" They were standing all the way to the second El post, and when the cops asked for witnesses none of them except Mrs. Oliver offered to give their names. Then Syl looked at Pa and me and saw our faces and turned to the crowd and began to scream.

"In another few years, you wait! Some of you are working people and they'll be marching through the streets and going after you too! They pick on us Jews because we're weak and haven't any country; but after they get us down they'll go after you! And it'll be your fault; you're all cowards, you're afraid to fight back!"

"Listen," one of the cops told my sister, "are you coming to the station or not? We can't hang around here all evening."

Then Syl broke down and began to bawl as hard as me. "Oh, leave us alone," she told them and began wailing her heart out. "Leave us alone. What good would it do?"

By this time the crowd was bigger, so the cops started telling people to break it up and move on. Nick came out and took my father by the arm into the lunchroom for a drink of hot tea. The people went away slowly and then, as the crowd began to dwindle, it started to snow. When she saw that, Syl started bawling harder than ever and turned her face to me. But I was down on my hands and knees with Mrs. Oliver, trying to save some of the magazines. There was no use going after the newspapers, which were smeared up, torn, and dirty from the gang's feet. But I thought I could save a few, so I picked a couple of them up.

"Oh, leave them be," Syl wept at me. "Leave them be, leave them be!"

A & P

by John Updike

IN WALKS these three girls in nothing but bathing suits. I'm in the third checkout slot, with my back to the door, so I don't see them until they're over by the bread. The one that caught my eye first was the one in the plaid green two-piece. She was a chunky kid, with a good tan and a sweet broad soft-looking can with those two crescents of white just under it, where the sun never seems to hit, at the top of the backs of her legs. I stood there with my hand on a box of HiHo crackers trying to remember if I rang it up or not. I ring it up again and the customer starts giving me hell. She's one of these cash-register-watchers, a witch about fifty with rouge on her cheekbones and no eyebrows, and I know it made her day to trip me up. She'd been watching cash registers for fifty years and probably never seen a mistake before.

By the time I got her feathers smoothed and her goodies into a bag—she gives me a little snort in passing, if she'd been born at the right time they would have burned her over in Salem—by the time I get her on her way the girls had circled around the bread and were coming back, without a pushcart, back my way along the counters, in the aisle between the checkouts and the Special bins. They didn't even have shoes on. There was this chunky one, with the two-piece—it was bright green and the seams on the bra were still sharp and her belly was still pretty pale so I guessed she just got it (the suit)—there was this one, with one of those chubby berry-faces, the lips all bunched together under her nose, this one, and a tall one, with black

hair that hadn't quite frizzed right, and one of these sun-
burns right across under the eyes, and a chin that was too
long—you know, the kind of girl other girls think is very
"striking" and "attractive" but never quite makes it, as
they very well know, which is why they like her so much—
and then the third one, that wasn't quite so tall. She was
the queen. She kind of led them, the other two peeking
around and making their shoulders round. She didn't look
around, not this queen, she just walked straight on slowly,
on these long white prima-donna legs. She came down a
little hard on her heels, as if she didn't walk in her bare
feet that much, putting down her heels and then letting the
weight move along to her toes as if she was testing the floor
with every step, putting a little deliberate extra action into
it. You never know for sure how girls' minds work (do
you really think it's a mind in there or just a little buzz
like a bee in a glass jar?) but you got the idea she had
talked the other two into coming in here with her, and
now she was showing them how to do it, walk slow and
hold yourself straight.

She had on a kind of dirty-pink—beige maybe, I
don't know—bathing suit with a little nubble all over it
and, what got me, the straps were down. They were off
her shoulders looped loose around the cool tops of her
arms, and I guess as a result the suit had slipped a little
on her, so all around the top of the cloth there was this
shining rim. If it hadn't been there you wouldn't have
known there could have been anything whiter than those
shoulders. With the straps pushed off, there was nothing
between the top of the suit and the top of her head except
just *her*, this clean bare plane of the top of her chest down
from the shoulder bones like a dented sheet of metal tilted
in the light. I mean, it was more than pretty.

She had sort of oaky hair that the sun and salt had
bleached, done up in a bun that was unravelling, and a
kind of prim face. Walking into the A & P with your
straps down, I suppose it's the only kind of face you *can*
have. She held her head so high her neck, coming up out

of those white shoulders, looked kind of stretched, but I didn't mind. The longer her neck was, the more of her there was.

She must have felt in the corner of her eye me and over my shoulder Stokesie in the second slot watching, but she didn't tip. Not this queen. She kept her eyes moving across the racks, and stopped, and turned so slow it made my stomach rub the inside of my apron, and buzzed to the other two, who kind of huddled against her for relief, and then they all three of them went up the cat-and-dog-food-breakfast-cereal-macaroni-rice-raisins-seasoning-spreads-spaghetti-soft-drinks-crackers-and-cookies aisle. From the third slot I look straight up this aisle to the meat counter, and I watched them all the way. The fat one with the tan sort of fumbled with the cookies, but on second thought she put the package back. The sheep pushing their carts down the aisle—the girls were walking against the usual traffic (not that we have one-way signs or anything)—were pretty hilarious. You could see them, when Queenie's white shoulders dawned on them, kind of jerk, or hop, or hiccup, but their eyes snapped back to their own baskets and on they pushed. I bet you could set off dynamite in an A & P and the people would by and large keep reaching and checking oatmeal off their lists and muttering "Let me see, there was a third thing, began with A, asparagus, no, ah, yes, apple-sauce!" or whatever it is they do mutter. But there was no doubt, this jiggled them. A few houseslaves in pin curlers even looked around after pushing their carts past to make sure what they had seen was correct.

You know, it's one thing to have a girl in a bathing suit down on the beach, where what with the glare nobody can look at each other much anyway, and another thing in the cool of the A & P, under the fluorescent lights, against all those stacked packages, with her feet paddling along naked over our checkerboard green-and-cream rubber-tile floor.

"Oh Daddy," Stokesie said beside me. "I feel so faint."

"Darling," I said. "Hold me tight." Stokesie's married, with two babies chalked up on his fuselage already, but as far as I can tell that's the only difference. He's twenty-two, and I was nineteen this April.

"Is it done?" he asks, the responsible married man finding his voice. I forgot to say he thinks he's going to be manager some sunny day, maybe in 1990 when it's called the Great Alexandrov and Petrooshki Tea Company or something.

What he meant was, our town is five miles from a beach, with a big summer colony out on the Point, but we're right in the middle of town, and the women generally put on a shirt or shorts or something before they get out of the car into the street. And anyway these are usually women with six children and varicose veins mapping their legs and nobody, including them, could care less. As I say, we're right in the middle of town, and if you stand at our front doors you can see two banks and the Congregational church and the newspaper store and three real-estate offices and about twenty-seven old freeloaders tearing up Central Street because the sewer broke again. It's not as if we're on the Cape; we're north of Boston and there's people in this town haven't seen the ocean for twenty years.

The girls had reached the meat counter and were asking McMahon something. He pointed, they pointed, and they shuffled out of sight behind a pyramid of Diet Delight peaches. All that was left for us to see was old McMahon patting his mouth and looking after them sizing up their joints. Poor kids, I began to feel sorry for them, they couldn't help it.

Now here comes the sad part of the story, at least my family says it's sad, but I don't think it's so sad myself. The store's pretty empty, it being Thursday afternoon, so there was nothing much to do except lean on the register and wait for the girls to show up again. The whole store was like a pinball machine and I didn't know which tunnel they'd come out of. After a while they come around out of the far aisle, around the light bulbs, records at discount of the Caribbean Six or Tony Martin Sings or some such gunk you wonder they waste the wax on, sixpacks of candy bars, and plastic toys done up in cellophane that fall apart when a kid looks at them anyway. Around they come, Queenie still leading the way, and holding a little gray jar in her hand. Slots Three through Seven are unmanned and I could see her wondering between Stokes and me, but Stokesie with his usual luck draws an old party in baggy gray pants who stumbles up with four giant cans of pineapple juice (what do these bums *do* with all that pineapple juice? I've often asked myself) so the girls come to me. Queenie puts down the jar and I take it into my fingers icy cold. Kingfish Fancy Herring Snacks in Pure Sour Cream: 49¢. Now her hands are empty, not a ring or a bracelet, bare as God made them, and I wonder where the money's coming from. Still with that prim look she lifts a folded dollar bill out of the hollow at the center of her nubbled pink top. The jar went heavy in my hand. Really, I thought that was so cute.

Then everybody's luck begins to run out. Lengel comes in from haggling with a truck full of cabbages on the lot and is about to scuttle into that door marked MANAGER behind which he hides all day when the girls touch his eye. Lengel's pretty dreary, teaches Sunday school and the rest, but he doesn't miss that much. He comes over and says, "Girls, this isn't the beach."

Queenie blushes, though maybe it's just a brush of sunburn I was noticing for the first time, now that she was so close. "My mother asked me to pick up a jar of herring snacks." Her voice kind of startled me, the way voices do when you see the people first, coming out so flat and dumb yet kind of tony, too, the way it tickled over "pick up" and "snacks." All of a sudden I slid right down her voice into her living room. Her father and the other men were standing around in ice-cream coats and bow ties and the women were in sandals picking up herring snacks on toothpicks off a big glass plate and they were all holding drinks the color of water with olives and sprigs of mint in them. When my parents have somebody over they get lemonade

and if it's a real racy affair Schlitz in tall glasses with
"They'll Do It Every Time" cartoons stencilled on.

"That's all right," Lengel said. "But this isn't the beach."
His repeating this struck me as funny, as if it had just
occurred to him, and he had been thinking all these years
the A & P was a great big dune and he was the head life-
guard. He didn't like my smiling—as I say he doesn't miss
much—but he concentrates on giving the girls that sad
Sunday-school-superintendent stare.

Queenie's blush is no sunburn now, and the plump one
in plaid, that I like better from the back—a really sweet
can—pipes up, "We weren't doing any shopping. We just
came in for the one thing."

"That makes no difference," Lengel tells her, and I
could see from the way his eyes went that he hadn't noticed
she was wearing a two-piece before. "We want you decently
dressed when you come in here."

"We *are* decent," Queenie says suddenly, her lower lip
pushing, getting sore now that she remembers her place, a
place from which the crowd that runs the A & P must look
pretty crummy. Fancy Herring Snacks flashed in her very
blue eyes.

"Girls, I didn't want to argue with you. After this come
in here with your shoulders covered. It's our policy." He
turns his back. That's policy for you. Policy is what the
kingpins want. What the others want is juvenile delin-
quency.

All this while, the customers had been showing up with
their carts but, you know, sheep, seeing a scene, they had
all bunched up on Stokesie, who shook open a paper bag
as gently as peeling a peach, not wanting to miss a word.
I could feel in the silence everybody getting nervous, most
of all Lengel, who asks me, "Sammy, have you rung up
their purchase?"

I thought and said "No" but it wasn't about that I was
thinking. I go through the punches, 4, 9, GROC, TOT—it's
more complicated than you think, and after you do it often
enough, it begins to make a little song, that you hear words
to, in my case "Hello (*bing*) there, you (*gung*) hap-py

pee-pul (*splat*)!"—the *splat* being the drawer flying out.
I uncrease the bill, tenderly as you may imagine, it just
having come from between the two smoothest scoops of
vanilla I had ever known were there, and pass a half and a
penny into her narrow pink palm, and nestled the herrings
in a bag and twist its neck and hand it over, all the time
thinking.

The girls, and who'd blame them, are in a hurry to get
out, so I say "I quit" to Lengel quick enough for them to
hear, hoping they'll stop and watch me, their unsuspected
hero. They keep right on going, into the electric eye; the
door flies open and they flicker across the lot to their car,
Queenie and Plaid and Big Tall Goony-Goony (not that
as raw material she was so bad), leaving me with Lengel
and a kink in his eyebrow.

"Did you say something, Sammy?"

"I said I quit."

"I thought you did."

"You didn't have to embarrass them."

"It was they who were embarrassing us."

I started to say something that came out "Fiddle-de-
doo." It's a saying of my grandmother's, and I know she
would have been pleased.

"I don't think you know what you're saying," Lengel
said.

"I know you don't," I said. "But I do." I pull the bow
at the back of my apron and start shrugging it off my
shoulders. A couple customers that had been heading for
my slot begin to knock against each other, like scared
pigs in a chute.

Lengel sighs and begins to look very patient and old
and gray. He's been a friend of my parents for years.
"Sammy, you don't want to do this to your Mom and
Dad," he tells me. It's true, I don't. But it seems to me
that once you begin a gesture it's fatal not to go through
with it. I fold the apron, "Sammy" stitched in red on the
pocket, and put it on the counter, and drop the bow tie on
top of it. The bow tie is theirs, if you've ever wondered.
"You'll feel this for the rest of your life," Lengel says,

and I know that's true, too, but remembering how he made that pretty girl blush makes me so scrunchy inside I punch the No Sale tab and the machine whirs "pee-pul" and the drawer splats out. One advantage to this scene taking place in summer, I can follow this up with a clean exit, there's no fumbling around getting your coat and galoshes, I just saunter into the electric eye in my white shirt that my mother ironed the night before, and the door heaves itself open, and outside the sunshine is skating around on the asphalt.

I look around for my girls, but they're gone, of course. There wasn't anybody but some young married screaming with her children about some candy they didn't get by the door of a powder-blue Falcon station wagon. Looking back in the big windows, over the bags of peat moss and aluminum lawn furniture stacked on the pavement, I could see Lengel in my place in the slot, checking the sheep through. His face was dark gray and his back stiff, as if he'd just had an injection of iron, and my stomach kind of fell as I felt how hard the world was going to be to me hereafter.

PHONE CALL

by Berton Roueché

I GOT OUT OF THE TRUCK and got down on my knees and twisted my neck and looked underneath. Everything looked O.K. There wasn't anything hanging down or anything. I got up and opened the hood and looked at the engine. I don't know too much about engines—only what I picked up working around Lindy's Service Station the summer before last. But the engine looked O.K., too. I slammed down the hood and lighted a cigarette. It really had me beat. A school bus from that convent over in Sag Harbor came piling around the bend, and all the girls leaned out the windows and yelled. I just waved. They didn't mean anything by it—just a bunch of kids going home. The bus went on up the road and into the woods and out of sight. I got back in the truck and started it up again. It sounded fine. I put it in gear and let out the clutch and gave it the gas, and nothing happened. The bastard just sat there. So it was probably the transmission. I shut it off and got out. There was nothing to do but call the store. I still had three or four deliveries that had to be made and it was getting kind of late. I knew what Mr. Lester would say, but this was one time when he couldn't blame me. It wasn't my fault. It was him himself that told me to take this truck.

There was a house just up the road—a big white house at the edge of the woods, with a white Rambler station wagon standing in the drive. I dropped my cigarette in a pothole puddle and started up the road, and stopped. A dog was laying there in the grass beside the station wagon. It put up its head and—oh, Jesus! it was one of those German police dogs. I turned around and headed the other way. There was another house back there around the bend. I remembered passing it. I went by the truck and walked down the road and around the bend, and the house was there. It was a brown shingle house with red shutters, and there was a sign in one of the windows: "Piano Lessons." The name on the mailbox was Timothy. I couldn't tell if there was anybody home or not. There wasn't any car around, but there was a garage at the end of the drive, and it could be parked in there. I went up the drive and around to the kitchen door, and when I got close I could hear a radio talking and laughing inside. I knocked on the door.

The radio went off. Then the door opened a crack and a woman looked out. She had bright blond hair and little black eyes, and she was forty years old at least. "Yes?" she said.

"Mrs. Timothy?" I said. "I work for the market over in Bridgehampton, Mrs. Timothy, and my truck—"

"How do you know my name?" she said.

"What?" I said. "Why—it's on the mailbox. I just read it on the mailbox."

"Oh," she said. She licked her lips. "And you say you work for a market?"

"That's right," I said. "The market over in Bridgehampton. And my truck's broke down. So I wondered—"

"What market?" she said.

"Why, Lester's Market," I said. "You know—over in Bridgehampton?"

"I see," she said.

"That's right," I said. "And my truck's broke down. I wondered could I use your phone to call the store and tell them?"

"Well," she said. She looked at me for about a minute. Then she stepped back and opened the door. She had on a pink sweater and one of those big, wide skirts with big, wide pockets, and she was nothing but skin and bones. "The telephone's in the living room. I'll show you."

I followed her through the kitchen and across a hall

into the living room. I guess that was where she gave her music lessons, too. There was a piano there against the wall and a music stand and a couple of folding chairs, and on top of the piano was a clarinet and one of those metronomes and a big pile of sheet music. The telephone was on a desk between the windows.

"I don't suppose you need the book?" Mrs. Timothy said.

"What?" I said.

"The telephone book," she said. "You know the number of your store, I hope?"

"Oh, sure," I said.

"Very well," she said. She reached up and straightened the "Piano Lessons" sign in the window. "Then go ahead and make your—"

She turned around, and she had the funniest look on her face. I mean, it was real strange. It was like she was scared or something.

"I thought you said you had a truck?" she said. "I don't see any truck out there."

"My truck?" I said. "Oh, it's up around the bend. That's where it broke down. You can't see it from here."

"I see," she said, and looked at me. She still had that funny look on her face. Even her voice sounded funny. "I'm here alone, but I want you to know something," she said. "I don't live alone. I'm married. I've got a husband, and he'll be home any minute. He gets off work early today." She came away from the window. "So my advice to you is to make your call just as quickly as you can."

"O.K.," I said, but I didn't get it. I watched her go across the room and through the hall to the kitchen. I didn't get it at all. She acted almost like I'd done something. I heard a car on the road and looked out. I thought maybe it might be her husband, but it was only some guys in a beat-up '59 Impala. But so what if it was her husband? I mean, Jesus—she really had me going. I turned back to the desk and picked up the phone. A woman's voice said, "But, of course, I never let on. I simply—"

I put down the phone and lighted a cigarette, and wandered down the room. I stopped at the piano and looked at the pile of sheet music. They were none of them songs I ever heard of. I looked around for an ashtray, and I found a big white clamshell. It looked like they used it for that. It was on a little table next to an easy chair. Then I went back and tried the phone again. The woman was still talking. I listened for a moment, but it sounded like she was still going strong. I was beginning to get kind of worried. I looked at my watch. It was already almost four o'clock. I went over to the clamshell and punched out my cigarette, but I guess I was in too big of a hurry. I punched too hard or something, and the clamshell flipped off the table. I made a grab, but I only touched it, and it skidded across the rug. I squatted down and picked it up, and, thank God, it wasn't broken. I must have broke its fall. It wasn't even cracked.

I heard Mrs. Timothy coming. The cigarette butt had rolled under the chair, and I brushed the ashes after it. Mrs. Timothy came through the door, and stopped. Her mouth fell open.

"It's O.K.," I said. "It didn't even—"

"What were you doing in that table drawer?" she said.

"What?" I said.

"I said what were you doing in that table drawer?" she said.

I shook my head. "Nothing," I said. "What drawer? I mean, I wasn't doing anything in any drawer. I just accidentally dropped this ashtray. I dropped it and I was just picking it up."

Mrs. Timothy didn't say anything. She just stood there and looked at me. Then she cleared her throat. "Well," she said. "Did you make your call?"

"Not yet," I said. "The line was busy."

"Oh?" she said. "And how do you know that? I didn't hear you dial or even say a word."

"I don't mean the store," I said. "I mean the party line. It was your line was busy."

She gave me one of those looks. Something sure was eating her. She walked over to the desk and picked up the phone and listened. Then she held it out. I could hear the buzz of the empty line. She put down the phone. "I suppose they just this minute hung up," she said. "Is that what I'm supposed to believe?"

"There was somebody talking before," I said. "I tried it twice."

"I don't know what you have in mind, but I advise you to forget it," she said. "I'm not that easily fooled. I'm really not as stupid as you seem to think. I know what's going on these days. I read the papers, you know. I hear the news, and I've heard about boys like you. I know all about them. I didn't want to let you in. I only did it against my better judgment. I had a feeling about you the minute I opened the door." She stood back against the desk. "I don't believe you had a breakdown. I don't believe it for a minute. If you broke down where you say you did, you were practically in front of the Millers', so that's where you would have gone to phone. You wouldn't have come all the way down here. I don't think you even *have* a truck. I think you came through the woods." She took a deep breath. "And now I want you to leave. I want you to get out of my house."

"I don't know what you're talking about, Mrs. Timothy," I said. "I just want to call the store. I've *got* to call the store."

"I said get out of my house," she said.

"O.K.," I said. "O.K., but—"

"I said get out," she said. She reached in one of the pockets of her big skirt and brought out a knife. It was a kitchen knife, with a long blade honed down thin. She pointed it at me like a gun.

"Hey!" I said.

"Oh, I see," she said. "That changes things. It's a different story now, isn't it? You didn't know I could take care of myself, did you? That never occurred to you." She came away from the desk. "You thought I was just another helpless woman, didn't you?"

I stepped back a couple of steps.

"Hey," I said. "For God's sake, what do you—"

"What's the matter?" she said. "You're not afraid of me, are you?" She moved the knife. "A big, strong, tough boy like you?"

I stepped back again.

"Hey," I said. "For God's sake, what do you—"

"You *are* a big, strong, tough boy," she said. "Aren't you?"

"For God's sake, Mrs. Timothy," I said. "I don't know what you're talking about. I wasn't doing anything."

She kind of smiled. "A great, big, strong, tough boy," she said.

I didn't say anything. The way she was looking at me, I couldn't hardly think, I couldn't hardly even believe it. It was like it was all a dream. I took another step, and stumbled into one of the folding chairs. Then I was up against the piano. I looked at that knife coming at me and my heart began to jump. She meant it. She really meant it, but that didn't mean I had to just stand there and let her. I slid along the front of the piano and reached up and touched the metronome and pushed it away and stretched and found the clarinet and grabbed it.

She let out a kind of yell. "Don't you dare!" she said. "You put that down!" She raised the knife. "Put that clarinet down."

But I had a good grip on it now. I looked at that knife with the point coming at me, and swung. I swung at it as hard as I could. I felt it connect, it tingled all the way up my arm. The knife went sailing across the room and I heard it hit the wall. Mrs. Timothy didn't move. She just stood there, and she was holding her wrist. It wasn't bleeding or anything, but it looked kind of funny and loose. Then she began to scream.

THE FIRST DEATH OF HER LIFE

by Elizabeth Taylor

SUDDENLY, tears poured from Lucy's eyes. She rested her forehead against her mother's hand and let the tears soak into the counterpane.

Dear Mr. Wilcox, she began, for her mind was always composing letters, I shall not be at the shop for the next four days, as my mother has passed away and I shall not be available until after the funeral. My mother passed away very peacefully. . . .

The nurse came in. She took her patient's wrist for a moment, replaced it on the bed, removed a jar of white lilac from the table, as if this were no longer necessary, and went out again.

The girl kneeling by the bed had looked up, but Dear Mr. Wilcox, she resumed, her eyes returning to the counterpane, My mother has died. I shall come back to work the day after tomorrow. Yours sincerely, Lucy Mayhew.

Her father was late. She imagined him hurrying from work, bicycling through the darkening streets, dogged, hunched up, slush thrown up by his wheels. Her mother did not move. Lucy stroked her mother's hand, with its loose gold ring, the calloused palm, the fine, long fingers. Then she stood up stiffly, her knees bruised from the waxed floor, and went to the window.

Snowflakes turned idly, drifting down over the hospital gardens. It was four o'clock in the afternoon and already the day seemed over. So few sounds came from this muffled and discolored world. In the hospital itself, there was a deep silence.

Her thoughts came to her in words, as if her mind spoke them first, understood them later. She tried to think of her childhood—little scenes she selected to prove how she and her mother had loved one another. Other scenes, especially last week's quarrel, she chose to forget, not knowing that in this moment she sent them away forever. Only loving-kindness remained. But, all the same, intolerable pictures broke through—her mother at the sink; her mother ironing; her mother standing between the lace curtains, staring out at the dreary street with a wounded look in her eyes; her mother tying the same lace curtains with yellow ribbons; attempts at lightness, gaiety, which came to nothing; her mother gathering her huge black cat to her, burying her face in its fur while a great, shivering sigh—of despair, of boredom—escaped her.

Her mother no longer sighed. She lay very still and sometimes took a little sip of air. Her arms were neatly at her side. Her eyes, which all day long had been turned to the white lilacs, were closed. Her cheekbones rose sharply from her bruised, exhausted face. She smelled faintly of wine. A small lilac flower floated on a glass of champagne, now discarded on the table at her side.

The champagne, with which they hoped to stretch out the thread of her life minute by minute, the lilac, the room of her own, all came to her at the end of a life of drabness and denial, just as, all along the mean street of the small English town where they lived, the dying and the dead were able to claim a lifetime's savings from the bereaved.

She is no longer there, Lucy thought, standing beside the bed. All day, her mother had stared at the white lilac; now she had sunk away. Outside, beyond the hospital gardens, mist settled over the town, blurred the street lamps.

The nurse returned with the matron. Lucy tautened, ready to be on her best behavior. In her heart, she trusted her mother to die without frightening her, and when the matron, deftly drawing Lucy's head to rest on her own shoulder, said in her calm voice, "She has gone," Lucy felt she had met this happening halfway.

A little bustle began, quick footsteps along the empty passages, and for a moment she was left alone with her dead mother. She laid her hand timidly on the soft, dark hair, so often touched, played with, when she was a child, standing on a stool behind her mother's chair while she sewed.

There were still the smell of wine and the hospital smell. It was growing dark in the room. She went to the dressing table and took her mother's handbag, very worn and shiny, and a book, a library book that she had chosen carefully, believing her mother would read it. Then she had a quick sip from the glass on the table, a mouthful of champagne, which she had never tasted before, and, looking wounded and aloof, walked down the middle of the corridor, feeling nurses falling away to left and right. Opening the glass doors onto the snowy gardens, she thought that it was like the end of a film. But no music rose up and engulfed her. Instead, there was her father turning in at the gates. He propped his bicycle against the wall and began to run clumsily across the wet gravel.

A COMPANY OF LAUGHING FACES

by Nadine Gordimer

WHEN KATHY HACK WAS SEVENTEEN her mother took her to Ingaza Beach for the Christmas holidays. The Hacks lived in the citrus-farming district of the Eastern Transvaal, and Kathy was an only child; "Mr. Hack wouldn't let me risk my life again," her mother confided at once, when ladies remarked, as they always did, that it was a lonely life when there was only one. Mrs. Hack usually added that she and her daughter were like sisters anyway; and it was true that since Kathy had left school a year ago she had led her mother's life, going about with her to the meetings and afternoon teas that occupied the ladies of the community. The community was one of retired business-men and mining officials from Johannesburg who had acquired fruit farms to give some semblance of produc-tivity to their leisure. They wore a lot of white linen and created a country-club atmosphere in the village where they came to shop. Mr. Hack had the chemist's shop there, but he too was in semi-retirement and he spent most of his afternoons on the golf course or in the club.

The village itself was like a holiday place, with its daz-zling white buildings and one wide street smelling of flowers; tropical trees threw shade and petals, and bou-gainvillaea climbed over the hotel. It was not a rest that Mrs. Hack sought at the coast, but a measure of gaiety and young company for Kathy. Naturally, there were few people under forty-five in the village and most of them had grown-up children who were married or away working or studying in the cities. Mrs. Hack couldn't be expected to part with Kathy—after all, she *is* the only one, she would explain—but, of course, she felt, the child must get out among youngsters once in a while. So she packed up and went on the two-day journey to the coast for Kathy's sake.

They travelled first class and Mrs. Hack had jokingly threatened Mr. Van Meulen, the station master, with dire consequences if he didn't see to it that they had a carriage to themselves. Yet though she had insisted that she wanted to read her book in peace and not be bothered with talking to some woman, the main-line train had hardly pulled out of Johannesburg station before she and Kathy edged their way along the train corridors to the dining car, and, over tea, Mrs. Hack at once got into conversation with the woman at the next table. There they sat for most of the afternoon; Kathy looking out of the window through the mist of human warmth and teapot steam in which she had drawn her name in with her forefinger and wiped a porthole with her fist, her mother talking gaily and comfortingly behind her. ". . . yes, a wonderful place for youngsters, they tell me. The kids really enjoy themselves there. . . . Well, of course, everything they want, dancing every night. Plenty of youngsters their own age, that's the thing. . . . *I* don't mind, I mean, I'm quite content to chat for half an hour and go off to my bed. . . ."

Kathy herself could not imagine what it would be like, this launching into the life of people her own age that her mother had in store for her; but her mother knew all about it and the idea was lit up inside the girl like a room made ready, with everything pulled straight and waiting. . . . Soon—very soon now, when they got there, when it all began to happen—life would set up in the room. She would know she was young. (When she was a little girl, she had often asked, but what is it like to *be* grown-up? She was too grown-up now to be able to ask, but what do you mean by "being young," "oh, to be young"—what is it *I* ought to feel?) Into the lit-up room would come the young people of her own age who would convey the secret quality of being that age; the dancing; the fun. She had the vaguest idea of what this fun would be; she had

danced, of course, at the monthly dances at the club, her
ear on a level with the strange breathing noises of middle-
aged partners who were winded by whisky. And the fun,
the fun? When she tried to think of it she saw a blur, a
company of laughing faces, the faces among balloons in
a Mardi Gras film, the crowd of bright-skinned, bright-
eyed faces like glazed fruits, reaching for a bottle of Coca-
Cola on a roadside hoarding.

The journey passed to the sound of her mother's voice.
When she was not talking, she looked up from time to
time from her knitting, and smiled at Kathy as if to remind
her. But Kathy needed no reminder; she thought of the
seven new dresses and the three new pairs of shorts in the
trunk in the van.

When she rattled up the dusty carriage shutters in the
morning and saw the sea, all the old wild joy of childhood
gushed in on her for a moment—the sight came to her as
the curl of the water along her ankles and the particular
sensation, through her hands, of a wooden spade lifting a
wedge of wet sand. But it was gone at once. It was the
past. For the rest of the day, she watched the sea approach
and depart, approach and depart as the train swung
towards and away from the shore through green bush and
sugar cane, and she was no more aware of it than her
mother, who, without stirring, had given the token recognition that Kathy had heard from her year after year as
a child: "Ah, I can smell the sea."

The hotel was full of mothers with their daughters. The
young men, mostly students, had come in groups of two or
three on their own. The mothers kept "well out of the
way," as Mrs. Hack enthusiastically put it; kept, in fact,
to their own comfortable adult preserve—the veranda and
the card room—and their own adult timetable—an early,
quiet breakfast before the young people, who had been out
till all hours, came in to make the dining room restless; a
walk or a chat, followed by a quick bathe and a quick
retreat from the hot beach back to the cool of the hotel; a
long sleep in the afternoon; bridge in the evening. Any
young person who appeared among them longer than to

snatch a kiss and fling a casual good-bye between one
activity and the next was treated with tolerant smiles and
jolly remarks that did not conceal a feeling that she really
ought to run off—she was there to enjoy herself wasn't she?
For the first few days Kathy withstood this attitude
stolidly; she knew no one and it seemed natural that she
should accompany her mother. But her mother made
friends at once, and Kathy became a hanger-on, something
her schoolgirl ethics had taught her to despise. She no
longer followed her mother onto the veranda. "Well, where
are you off to, darling?" "Up to change." She and her
mother paused in the foyer; her mother was smiling, as if
she caught a glimpse of the vista of the morning's youth-
ful pleasures. "Well, don't be too late for lunch. All the
best salads go first." "No, I won't." Kathy went evenly up
the stairs, under her mother's eyes.

In her room, that she shared with her mother, she undressed slowly and put on the new bathing suit. And the
new Italian straw hat. And the new sandals. And the new
bright wrap, printed with sea horses. The disguise worked
perfectly; she saw in the mirror a young woman like all
the others: she felt the blessed thrill of belonging. This
was the world for which she had been brought up, and
now, sure enough, when the time had come, she looked
the part. Yet it was a marvel to her, just as it must be to
the novice when she puts her medieval hood over her
shaved head and suddenly is a nun.

She went down to the beach and lay all morning close by,
but not part of, the groups of boys and girls who crowded
it for two hundred yards, lying in great ragged circles that
were constantly broken up and re-formed by chasing and
yelling, and the restless to-and-fro of those who were always getting themselves covered with sand in order to
make going into the water worth while, or coming back
out of the sea to fling a wet head down in someone's warm
lap. Nobody spoke to her except two huge louts who
tripped over her ankles and exclaimed a hoarse, "Gee, I'm
sorry"; but she was not exactly lonely—she had the satisfaction of knowing that at least she was where she ought

to be, down there on the beach with the young people.

Every day she wore another of the new dresses or the small tight shorts—properly, equipment rather than clothes —with which she had been provided. The weather was sufficiently steamy hot to be described by her mother, sitting deep in the shade of the veranda, as glorious. When, at certain moments, there was that pause that comes in the breathing of the sea, music from the beach tearoom wreathed up to the hotel, and at night, when the dance was in full swing down there, the volume of music and voices joined the volume of the sea's sound itself, so that, lying in bed in the dark, you could imagine yourself under the sea, with the waters sending swaying sound waves of sunken bells and the cries of drowned men ringing out from depth to depth long after they themselves have touched bottom in silence.

She exchanged smiles with other girls, on the stairs; she made a fourth, at tennis; but these encounters left her again, just exactly where they had taken her up—she scarcely remembered the mumbled exchange of names, and their owners disappeared back into the anonymous crowd of sprawled bare legs and sandals that filled the hotel. After three days, a young man asked her to go dancing with him at the Coconut Grove, a rickety bungalow on piles above the lagoon. There was to be a party of eight or more—she didn't know. The idea pleased her mother; it was just the sort of evening she liked to contemplate for Kathy. A jolly group of youngsters and no nonsense about going off in "couples."

The young man was in his father's wholesale tea business; "Are you at varsity?" he asked her, but seemed to have no interest in her life once that query was settled. The manner of dancing at the Coconut Grove was energetic and the thump of feet beat a continuous talc-like dust out of the wooden boards. It made the lights twinkle, as they do at twilight. Dutifully, every now and then the face of Kathy's escort, who was called Manny and was fair, with a spongy nose and small far-apart teeth in a wide grin, would appear close to her through the bright dust and he would dance with her. He danced with every girl in turn, picking them out and returning them to the pool again with obvious enjoyment and a happy absence of discrimination. In the intervals, Kathy was asked to dance by other boys in the party; sometimes a bold one from some other party would come up, run his eye over the girls, and choose one at random, just to demonstrate an easy confidence. Kathy felt helpless. Here and there there were girls who did not belong to the pool, boys who did not rove in predatory search simply because it was necessary to have a girl to dance with. A boy and a girl sat with hands loosely linked, and got up to dance time and again without losing this tenuous hold of each other. They talked, too. There was a lot of guffawing and some verbal sparring at the table where Kathy sat, but she found that she had scarcely spoken at all, the whole evening. When she got home and crept into bed in the dark, in order not to waken her mother, she was breathless from dancing all night, but she felt that she had been running, a long way, alone, with only the snatches of voices from memory in her ears.

She did everything everyone else did, now, waking up each day as if to a task. She had forgotten the anticipation of this holiday that she had had; that belonged to another life. It was gone, just as surely as what the sea used to be was gone. The sea was a shock of immersion in cold water, nothing more, in the hot sandy morning of sticky bodies, cigarette smoke, giggling, and ragging. Yet inside her was something distressing, akin to the thickness of not being able to taste when you have a cold. She longed to break through the muffle of automatism with which she carried through the motions of pleasure. There remained in her a desperate anxiety to succeed in being young, to grasp, not merely fraudulently to do, what was expected of her.

People came and went, in the life of the hotel, and their going was not noticed much. They were replaced by others much like them or who became like them, as those who enter into the performance of a rite inhabit a personality and a set of actions preserved in changeless continuity by

the rite itself. She was lying on the beach one morning in a
crowd when a young man dropped down beside her, turning his head quickly to see if he had puffed sand into her
face, but not speaking to her. She had seen him once or
twice before; he had been living at the hotel for two or
three days. He was one of those young men of the type
who are noticed; he no sooner settled down, lazily smoking, addressing some girl with exaggerated endearments
and supreme indifference, than he would suddenly get up
again and drop in on some other group. There he would be
seen in the same sort of ease and intimacy; the first group
would feel both slighted and yet admiring. He was not
dependent upon anyone; he gave or withheld his presence
as he pleased, and the mood of any gathering lifted a little
when he was there, simply because his being there was always unexpected. He had brought to perfection the art,
fashionable among the boys that year, of leading a girl to
believe that he had singled her out for his attention, "fallen
for her," and then, the second she acknowledged this,
destroying her self-confidence by one look or sentence
that made it seem that she had stupidly imagined the whole
thing.

Kathy was not surprised that he did not speak to her; she
knew only too well that she did not belong to that special
order of girls and boys among whom life was really
shared out, although outwardly the whole crowd might
appear to participate. It was going to be a very hot day;
already the sea was a deep, hard blue and the sky was
taking on the gauzy look of a mirage. The young man—his
back was half turned to her—had on a damp pair of
bathing trunks and on a level with her eyes, as she lay, she
could see a map-line of salt emerging white against the
blue material as the moisture dried out of it. He got into
some kind of argument, and his gestures released from
his body the smell of oil. The argument died down and
then, in relief at a new distraction, there was a general
move up to the beach tearoom where the crowd went every
day to drink variously coloured bubbly drinks and to dance,
in their bathing suits, to the music of a gramophone. It

was the usual straggling procession; "Aren't you fellows coming?"—the nasal, complaining voice of a girl. "Just a sec, what's happened to my glasses? . . ." "All right, don't *drag* me, man—" "Look what you've done!" "I don't want any more blisters, thank you very much, not after last night. . . ." Kathy lay watching them troop off, taking her time about following. Suddenly there was a space of sand in front of her, kicked up and tousled, but empty. She felt the sun, that had been kept off her right shoulder by the presence of the young man, strike her; he had got up to follow the others. She lay as if she had not heard when suddenly he was standing above her and had said, shortly, "Come for a walk." Her eyes moved anxiously. "Come for a walk," he said, taking out of his mouth the empty pipe that he was sucking. She sat up; going for a walk might have been something she had never done before, was not sure if she could do.

"I know you like walking."

She remembered that when she and some others had limped into the hotel from a hike the previous afternoon, he had been standing at the reception desk, looking up something in a directory. "All right," she said, subdued, and got up.

They walked quite briskly along the beach together. It was much cooler down at the water's edge. It was cooler away from the crowded part of the beach, too; soon they had left it behind. Each time she opened her mouth to speak, a mouthful of refreshing air came in. He did not bother with small talk—not even to the extent of an exchange of names. (Perhaps, despite his air of sophistication, he was not really old enough to have acquired any small talk. Kathy had a little stock, like premature grey hairs, that she had found quite useless at Ingaza Beach.) He was one of those people whose conversation is an interior monologue that now and then is made audible to others. There was a ship stuck like a tag out at sea, cut in half by the horizon, and he speculated about it, its size in relation to the distance, interrupting himself with thrown-away remarks, sceptical of his own speculation, that sometimes were left unfinished. He mentioned something an anonymous "they" had done "in the lab"; she said, taking the opportunity to take part in the conversation, "What do you do?"

"Going to be a chemist," he said.

She laughed with pleasure. "So's my father!"

He passed over the revelation and went on comparing the performance of an MG sports on standard commercial petrol with the performance of the same model on a special experimental mixture. "It's a lot of tripe, anyway," he said suddenly, abandoning the plaything of the subject. "Crazy fellows tearing up the place. What for?" As he walked he made a rhythmical clicking sound with his tongue on the roof of his mouth, in time to some tune that must have been going round in his head. She chattered intermittently and politely, but the only part of her consciousness that was acute was some small marginal awareness that along this stretch of gleaming, sloppy sand he was walking without making any attempt to avoid treading on the dozens of small spiral-shell creatures who sucked themselves down into the ooze at the shadow of an approach.

They came to the headland of rock that ended the beach. The rocks were red and smooth, the backs of centuries-warm, benign beasts; then a gaping black seam, all crenellated with turban-shells as small and rough as crumbs, ran through a rocky platform that tilted into the gnashing, hissing sea. A small boy was fishing down there, and he turned and looked after them for a few moments, perhaps expecting them to come to see what he had caught. But when they got to the seam, Kathy's companion stopped, noticed her; something seemed to occur to him; there was the merest suggestion of a pause, a reflex of a smile softened the corner of his mouth. He picked her up in his arms, not without effort, and carried her across. As he set her on her feet she saw his unconcerned eyes, and they changed, in her gaze, to the patronizing, pre-occupied expression of a grown-up who has swung a child in the air. The next time they came to a small obstacle, he stopped again, jerked his head in dry command, and picked her up again, though she could quite easily have stepped across the gap herself. This time they laughed, and she examined her arm when he had put her down. "It's awful, to be grabbed like that, without warning." She felt suddenly at ease, and wanted to linger at the rock pools, poking about in the tepid water for seaweed and the starfish that felt, as she ventured to tell him, exactly like a cat's tongue. "I wouldn't know," he said, not unkindly. "I haven't got a cat. Let's go." And they turned back towards the beach. But at anything that could possibly be interpreted as an obstacle, he swung her carelessly into his arms and carried her to safety. He did not laugh again, and so she did not either; it seemed to be some very serious game of chivalry. When they were down off the rocks, she ran into the water and butted into a wave and then came flying up to him with the usual shudders and squeals of complaint at the cold. He ran his palm down her bare back and said with distaste, "Ugh. What did you do that for."

And so they went back to the inhabited part of the beach and continued along the path up to the hotel, slowly returning to that state of anonymity, that proximity without contact, that belonged to the crowd. It was true, in fact, that she still did not know his name, and did not like to ask. Yet as they passed the beach tearoom, and heard the shuffle of bare sandy feet accompanying the wail and fall of a howling song, she had a sudden friendly vision of the dancers.

After lunch was the only time when the young people were in possession of the veranda. The grown-ups had gone up to sleep. There was an unwritten law against afternoon sleep for the young people; to admit a desire for sleep would have been to lose at once your fitness to be one of the young crowd: "Are you crazy?" The enervation of exposure to the long hot day went on without remission.

It was so hot, even in the shade of the veranda, that the heat seemed to increase gravity; legs spread, with more than their usual weight, on the grass chairs, feet rested heavily as the monolithic feet of certain sculptures. The young man sat beside Kathy, constantly relighting his pipe; she did not know whether he was bored with her or seeking out her company, but presently he spoke to her monosyllabically, and his laconicism was that of long familiarity. They dawdled down into the garden, where the heat was hardly any worse. There was bougainvillaea, as there was at home in the Eastern Transvaal—a huge, harsh shock of purple, papery flowers that had neither scent nor texture, only the stained-glass colour through which the light shone violently. Three boys passed with swinging rackets and screwed-up eyes, on their way to the tennis courts. Someone called, "Have you seen Micky and them?"

Then the veranda and garden were deserted. He lay with closed eyes on the prickly grass and stroked her hand—without being aware of it, she felt. She had never been caressed before, but she was not alarmed because it seemed to her such a simple gesture, like stroking a cat or a dog. She and her mother were great readers of novels and she knew, of course, that there were a large number of caresses—hair, and eyes and arms and even breasts—and an immense variety of feelings that would be attached to them. But this simple caress sympathized with her in the heat; she was so hot that she could not breathe with her lips closed and there was on her face a smile of actual suffering. The buzz of a fly round her head, the movement of a leggy red ant on the red earth beneath the grass made her aware that there were no voices, no people about; only the double presence of herself and the unknown person breathing beside her. He propped himself on his elbow and quickly put his half-open lips on her mouth. He gave her no time for surprise or shyness, but held her there, with his wet warm mouth; her instinct to resist the kiss with some part of herself—inhibition, inexperience—died away with the first ripple of its impulse, was smoothed and lost in the melting, boundaryless quality of physical being in the hot afternoon. The salt taste that was in the kiss— it was the sweat on his lip or on hers; his cheek, with its stipple of roughness beneath the surface, stuck to her cheek as the two surfaces of her own skin stuck together wherever they met. When he stood up, she rose obediently. The air seemed to swing together, between them. He put his arm across her shoulder—it was heavy and uncomfortable, and bent her head—and began to walk her along the path toward the side of the hotel.

"Come on," he said, barely aloud, as he took his arm away at the dark archway of an entrance. The sudden shade made her draw a deep breath. She stopped. "Where are you going?" He gave her a little urging push. "Inside," he said, looking at her. The abrupt change from light to dark affected her vision; she was seeing whorls and spots, her heart was plodding. Somewhere there was a moment's stay of uneasiness; but a great unfolding impulse, the blind turn of a daisy toward the sun, made her go calmly with him along the corridor, under his influence: her first whiff of the heady drug of another's will.

In a corridor of dark doors he looked quickly to left and right and then opened a door softly and motioned her in. He slipped in behind her and pushed home the old-fashioned bolt. Once it was done, she gave him a quick smile of adventure and complicity. The room was a bare little room, not like the one she shared with her mother. This was the old wing of the hotel, and it was certain that the push-up-and-down window did not have a view of the sea, although dingy striped curtains were drawn across it, anyway. The room smelled faintly of worn shoes, and the rather cold, stale, male smells of dead cigarette ends and ironed shirts; it was amazing that it could exist, so dim and forgotten, in the core of the hotel that took the brunt of a blazing sun. Yet she scarcely saw it; there was no chance to look round in the mood of curiosity that came upon her, like a movement down to earth. He stood in front of her, their bare thighs touching beneath their shorts, and kissed her and kissed her. His mouth was different then, it was cool, and she could feel it, delightfully, separate from her own. She became aware of the most extraordinary sensation; her little breasts, that she had never thought of as having any sort of assertion of life of their own, were suddenly inhabited by two struggling trees of feeling, one thrusting up, uncurling, spreading, toward each nipple. And from his lips, it came, this sensation! From his lips! This person she had spoken to for the first time that morning. How pale and slow were the emotions engendered, over years of childhood, by other people, compared to this! You lost the sea, yes, but you found this. When he stopped kissing her she followed his mouth like a calf nuzzling for milk.

Suddenly he thrust his heavy knee between hers. It was a movement so aggressive that he might have hit her. She gave an exclamation of surprise and backed away, in his arms. It was the sort of exclamation that, in the context of situations she was familiar with, automatically brought a solicitous apology—an equally startled "I'm sorry! Did I hurt you!" But this time there was no apology. The man was fighting with her; *he did not care* that the big bone of his knee had bruised hers. They struggled clumsily, and she was pushed backwards and landed up sitting on the bed. He stood in front of her, flushed and burning-eyed, contained in an orbit of attraction strong as the colour of a flower, and he said in a matter-of-fact, reserved voice, "It's all right. I know what I'm doing. There'll be nothing for you to worry about." He went over to the chest of drawers, while she sat on the bed. Like a patient in a doctor's waiting room: the idea swept into her head. She got up and unbolted the door. "Oh no," she said, a whole horror of prosaicness enveloping her, "I'm going now." The back of the stranger's neck turned abruptly away from her. He faced her, smiling exasperatedly, with a sneer at himself. "I thought so. I thought that would happen." He came over and the kisses that she tried to avoid smeared her face. "What the hell did you come in here for then, hey? Why did you come?" In disgust, he let her go.

She ran out of the hotel and through the garden down to the beach. The glare from the sea hit her, left and right, on both sides of her face; her face that felt battered out of shape by the experience of her own passion. She could not go back to her room because of her mother; the idea of her

mother made her furious. She was not thinking at all of
what had happened, but was filled with the idea of *her
mother*, lying there asleep in the room with a novel
dropped open on the bed. She stumbled off over the heavy
sand toward the rocks. Down there, there was nobody but
the figure of a small boy, digging things out of the wet sand
and putting them in a tin. She would have run from anyone, but he did not count; as she drew level with him, ten
yards off, he screwed up one eye against the sun and gave
her a crooked smile. He waved the tin. "I'm going to try
them for bait," he said. "See these little things?" She
nodded and walked on. Presently the child caught up with
her, slackening his pace conversationally. But they walked
on over the sand that the ebbing tide had laid smooth as a
tennis court, and he did not speak. He thudded his heels
into the firmness.

At last he said, "That was me, fishing on the rocks over
there this morning."

She said with an effort, "Oh, was it? I didn't recognize
you." Then, after a moment: "Did you catch anything?"

"Nothing much. It wasn't a good day." He picked a
spiral shell out of his tin and the creature within put out
a little undulating body like a flag. "I'm going to try these.
No harm in trying."

He was about nine years old, thin and hard, his hair and
face covered with a fine powder of salt—even his eyelashes
held it. He was at exactly the stage of equidistant remote-
ness: he had forgotten his mother's lap, and had no inkling
of the breaking voice and growing beard to come. She
picked one of the spirals out of the tin, and the creature
came out and furled and unfurled itself about her fingers.
He picked one of the biggest. "I'll bet this one'd win if we
raced them," he said. They went nearer the water and set
the creatures down when the boy gave the word "Go!"
When the creatures disappeared under the sand, they dug
them out with their toes. Progressing in this fashion, they
came to the rocks, and began wading about in the pools.
He showed her a tiny hermit crab that had blue eyes; she
thought it the most charming thing she had ever seen and

poked about until she found one like it for herself. They laid out on the rock five different colours of starfish, and discussed possible methods of drying them; he wanted to take back some sort of collection for the natural-history class at his school. After a time, he picked up his tin and said, with a responsible sigh, "Well, I better get on with my fishing." From the point of a particularly high rock, he turned to wave at her.

She walked along the water's edge back to the hotel. In the room, her mother was spraying cologne down the front of her dress. "Darling, you'll get boiled alive, going to the beach at this hour." "No," said Kathy, "I'm used to it now." When her mother had left the room, Kathy went to the dressing table to brush her hair, and running her tongue over her dry lips, tasted not the salt of the sea, but of sweat; it came to her as a dull reminder. She went into the bathroom and washed her face and cleaned her teeth, and then quietly powdered her face again.

Christmas was distorted, as by a thick lens, by swollen, rippling heat. The colours of paper caps ran on sweating foreheads. The men ate flaming pudding in their shirt-sleeves. Flies settled on the tinsel snow of the Christmas tree.

Dancing in the same room on Christmas Eve, Kathy and the young man ignored each other with newly acquired adult complicity. Night after night Kathy danced, and did not lack partners. Though it was not for Mrs. Hack to say it, the new dresses *were* a great success. There was no girl who looked nicer. "K. is having the time of her life," wrote Mrs. Hack to her husband. "Very much in the swing. She's come out of herself completely."

Certainly Kathy was no longer waiting for a sign; she had discovered that this was what it was to be young, of course, just exactly this life in the crowd that she had been living all along, silly little ass that she was, without knowing it. There it was. And once you'd got into it, well, you just went on. You clapped and booed with the others at the Sunday night talent contests, you pretended to kick sand in the boys' faces when they whistled at your legs; squashed into an overloaded car, you yelled songs as you drove, and knew that you couldn't have any trouble with a chap (on whose knees you found yourself) getting too fresh, although he could hold your hand adoringly. The thickness of skin required for all this came just as the required suntan did; and everyone was teak-brown, sallow-brown, homogenized into a new leathery race by the rigorous daily exposure to the fierce sun. The only need she had, these days, it seemed, was to be where the gang was; then the question of what to do and how to feel solved itself. The crowd was flat or the crowd was gay; they wanted to organize a beauty contest or trail to the beach at midnight for a watermelon feast.

One afternoon someone got up a hike to a small resort a few miles up the coast. This was the sort of jaunt in which brothers and sisters who really were still too young to qualify for the crowd were allowed to join; there were even a few children who tagged along. The place itself was strange, with a half-hidden waterfall, like a rope, and great tiers of overhanging rock stretching out farther and farther, higher and higher, over a black lagoon; the sun never reached the water. On the other side, where the sea ran into the lagoon at high tide, there was open beach, and there the restless migration from Ingaza Beach settled. Even there, the sand was cool; Kathy felt it soothing to her feet as she struggled out of the shorts and shirt she had worn over her bathing suit while she walked. She swam steadily about, dipping to swim underwater when the surface began to explode all over the place with the impact of the bodies of the boys who soon clambered up the easier reaches of rock and dived from them. People swam close under the wide roof of rock and looked up; hanging plants grew there, and the whole undersurface was chalky, against its rust-streaked blackness, with the droppings of swallows that threaded in and out of the ledges like bats. Kathy called out to someone from there and her voice came ringing down at her: ". . . al-l-low!" Soon the swimmers were back on the sand, wet and restless, to eat chocolate and smoke. Cold drinks were brought down by an Indian waiter from the little hotel overlooking the beach; two girls buried a boy up to the neck in sand; somebody came out of the water with a bleeding toe, cut on a rock. People went off exploring, there was always a noisy crowd clowning in the water, and there were always a few others lying about talking on the sand. Kathy was in such a group when one of the young men came up with his hands on his hips, lips drawn back from his teeth thoughtfully, and asked, "Have you seen the Bute kid around here?" "What kid?" someone said. "Kid about ten, in green trunks. Libby Bute's kid brother." "Oh, I know the one you mean. I don't know—all the little boys were playing around on the rocks over there, just now." The young man scanned the beach, nodding. "Nobody knows where he's got to."

"The kids were all together over there, only a minute ago."

"I know. But he can't be found. Kids say they don't know where he is. He might have gone fishing. But Libby says he would have told her. He was supposed to tell her if he went off on his own."

Kathy was making holes in the sand with her forefinger. "Is that the little boy who goes fishing up on the rocks at the end of our beach?"

"Mm. Libby's kid brother."

Kathy got up and looked round at the people, the lagoon, as if she were trying to reinterpret what she had seen before. "I didn't know he was here. I don't remember seeing him. With those kids who were fooling around with the birds' nests?"

"That's right. He was there." The young man made a little movement with his shoulders and wandered off to approach some people farther along. Kathy and her companions went on to talk of something else. But suddenly there was a stir on the beach; a growing stir. People were getting up; others were coming out of the water. The young man hurried past again; "He's not found," they caught from him in passing. People began moving about from one knot to another, gathering suppositions, hoping for news they'd missed. Centre of an awkward, solicitous, bossy circle was Libby Bute herself, a dark girl with long hands and a bad skin, wavering uncertainly between annoyance and fear. "I suppose the little tyke's gone off to fish somewhere, without a word. I don't know. Doesn't mean a thing that he didn't have his fishing stuff with him, he's always got a bit of string and a couple of pins." Nobody said anything. "He'll turn up," she said; and then looked round at them all.

An hour later, when the sun was already beginning to drop from its afternoon zenith, he was not found. Everyone was searching for him with a strange concentration, as if, in the mind of each one, an answer, the remembrance of where he was, lay undisturbed, if only one could get at it. Before there was time for dread, like doubt, like dew, to form coldly, Kathy Hack came face to face with him. She was crawling along the first ledge of rock because she had an idea he might have got it into his head to climb into what appeared to be a sort of cave behind the waterfall, and be stuck there, unable to get out and unable to make himself heard. She glanced down into the water, and saw a glimmer of light below the surface. She leant over between her haunches and he was looking at her, not more than a foot below the water, where, shallow over his face, it showed golden above its peat-coloured depths. The water was very deep there, but he had not gone far. He lay held up by the just-submerged rock that had struck the back of his head as he had fallen backwards into the lagoon. What she felt was not shock, but recognition. It was as if he had had a finger to his lips, holding the two of them there, so that she might not give him away. The water moved but did not move him; only his little bit of short hair was faintly obedient, leaning the way of the current, as the green beard of the rock did. He was as absorbed as he must have been in whatever it was he was doing when he fell. She looked at him, looked at him, for a minute, and then she clambered back to the shore and went on with the search. In a little while, someone else found him, and Libby Bute lay screaming on the beach, saliva and sand clinging round her mouth.

Two days later, when it was all over, and more than nine pounds had been collected among the hotel guests for a wreath, and the body was on the train to Johannesburg, Kathy said to her mother, "I'd like to go home." Their holiday had another week to run. "Oh I know," said Mrs. Hack with quick sympathy. "I feel the same myself. I can't get that poor little soul out of my mind. But life has to go on, darling, one can't take the whole world's troubles on one's shoulders. Life brings you enough troubles of your own, believe me." "It's not that at all," said Kathy. "I don't like this place."

Mrs. Hack was just feeling herself nicely settled, and would have liked another week. But she felt that there was the proof of some sort of undeniable superiority in her daughter's great sensitivity; a superiority they ought not to forgo. She told the hotel proprietor and the other mothers that she had to leave; that was all there was to it: Kathy was far too much upset by the death of the little stranger to be able simply to go ahead with the same zest for holiday pleasures that she had enjoyed up till now. Many young people could do it, of course; but not Kathy. She wasn't made that way, and what was she, her mother, to do about it?

In the train going home they did not have a carriage to themselves, and very soon Mrs. Hack was explaining to their lady travelling companion—in a low voice, between almost closed teeth, in order not to upset Kathy—how the marvellous holiday had been ruined by this awful thing that had happened.

The girl heard, but felt no impulse to tell her mother—knew, in fact, that she would never have the need to tell anyone the knowledge that had held her secure since the moment she looked down into the lagoon: the sight, there, was the one real happening of the holiday, the one truth and the one beauty.

THE ECLIPSE

by Elizabeth Enright

THAT JANUARY MORNING in 1925 was clear and cold. At seven-thirty the rising bell rang with its usual hellish brusqueness, and I huddled deeper in my bed trying to pretend sleep back again—trying to pretend, as I did every morning, that I need not get up until I wished. My three roommates were groaning lumps under the covers. The room was freezing; our breath was steam on the air, and the water in the glass beside my bed had turned to ice.

It was Nydia's turn to close the windows, but it was only after repeated insults and commands from the rest of us that she finally had the fortitude to hurl back the covers and make a majestic sprint, like a young Demeter in pajamas, to the casement windows.

"God!" she said, banging them shut. "Sweet God Almighty!" and she lunged back into bed.

Marcia reared up on her elbow and reached for her glasses. "God," she agreed. Then she yawned on a note of resignation and put her feet out, searching for her fur slippers which peered like a pair of hamsters from under the bed. "Well, kids, it has to be done," she said. Marcia had the twin advantages over the rest of us of being the most sensible and the most sophisticated. Many boys had kissed her and she had been invited to the Dartmouth Carnival.

Nydia, with her sapphire eyes, was the most beautiful; and Terry, who at this hour of the morning was still only a hump and a pigtail in her bed, was the richest, and was further set apart from the rest of us by the fact that she was seriously in love and was loved in return. She was always

receiving letters with such messages on the envelope-
flaps as "Wait and Hope," or "Darkest before Dawn," for
her love was starcrossed; her parents thought her far too
young for serious romance, and perhaps her wealth was an
obstacle, too.

As for me, I was the least sophisticated and the least
sensible, the least beautiful and the least rich; also I was
not in love. However, I thought fairly well of myself none
the less; the huge aurora borealis of adolescent hope
assured me that some day I would obtain these five major
requirements with very little trouble. They would just happen to me nicely when the time came.

Marcia slip-slapped back from the bathroom, looking
well-scrubbed and smelling of toothpaste.

"O.K., kids, up!" she said tersely. The two charac-
teristics mentioned, added to the fact that she was a trifle
older than the rest of us, endowed her with a quality of
leadership, almost of generalship, and sometimes she could
be ruthless. Now, for instance, she stooped and stripped the
covers away from Nydia. "Get up," she repeated, "today's the great day."

Seeing that peace was at an end I leaped out of bed,
and from Terry came sighs of slow upheaval. Terry had
brought four fur coats to school, and two of them—the
beaver, and the leopard with the red fox collar—were
draped on her bed as coverlets. More than any of us
she hated to get up in the morning, and often we con-
trived to sneak her breakfast to her, but today this was
out of the question.

"Who wants to see the damned old eclipse, anyway,"
she grumbled. But she grumbled amiably; she was never
really cross. She reached for the leopard coat and put it
on over her nightgown, then thrust her plump feet into the
high-heeled patent leather pumps she preferred to bedroom
slippers.

Nydia dressed silently. She was always silent and remote
before breakfast. I shivered and complained volubly, and
Marcia, butting her head into one of her many sweaters,
replied with comments deploring but philosophical.

The breakfast bell rang too soon. It always did. After that we were allowed five minutes leeway, and every day it was chaos and scuffle. This morning even Terry was goaded to haste.

"Where are my shoes, where are my damn shoes—oh, here . . . what did I put them on the bureau for?" she moaned distractedly.

Only Marcia was ready in plenty of time, neat in her skirt and sweater, her argyle-patterned wool stockings and saddle shoes. Nydia daringly applied some Roger & Gallet pink pomade to her lips, then rubbed it off again. She gave herself one last cold passionate look in the mirror and made a hook-shaped gesture with the palm of each hand against the blond sickle of hair that pressed against each cheek. At her side, sharing the mirror, I struggled with my own hair which I had pinned up for the first time a few months before. After weeks of practice I had succeeded in arranging it so that it looked more like cloth than hair. It was wrapped around my head in broad turban-bands. No hat would fit over it, and my scalp was stung with hairpins all day long, but I thought it looked handsome and unusual, though I cannot remember that anyone ever concurred in this opinion.

"Girls! Girls!" cried the house mother looking in at the door. "This is absolutely your last chance! Hurry!"

I cursed my turban of hair which, this morning, had turned out lopsided and rakish, but there was no time to change it. I plunged after my roommates who were already jostling and thundering down the stairs to the dining room where, for once, we could all enjoy a leisurely breakfast without thought of classes. Since there was to be a half-holiday in the universe, it was suitable that we should have one, too.

After breakfast was the time to straighten the rooms. We all made our own beds, and mine, when finished, looked rather lumpish due to the fact that the copy of *Wuthering Heights* that I had been reading the night before, by flashlight under the covers, was still in the bed. It is possible that the flashlight was there, too, though I have forgotten.

Each week one of us was delegated to do all the sweeping and dusting of the room, and this week it was my turn. My roommates departed heartlessly and I was left alone.

The room was large, with a bow of leaded casement windows and a window seat. The house and grounds had once been the estate of an heiress, and there was a certain grandeur about the size of everything, and the bathrooms were extremely luxurious for a boarding school. Most of the luxury and grandeur ended there, however. In our room there were two immense bureaus, and four narrow metal beds on which no two bedspreads were the same color or pattern. On the bureaus, among hair brushes and bottles of the kind of perfume people give teen-agers, the rather flattered photographs of parents and younger brothers looked out self-consciously. On the window seat there was a portable Victrola (we called it a "Vic"), a stack of records, many magazines, and a few stuffed animals. In the cabinet beneath the window seat there was, as I knew well, a jug of cider, which instead of turning hard was turning disappointingly to vinegar; there were several boxes of soda crackers, and a jar of Hyppolite marshmallow whip with a spoon in it. There may have been a bitten dill pickle in waxed paper—there often was—and there was almost certainly a pound box of salted peanuts. Tucked far back out of sight, beside the copy of *Flaming Youth*, and Balzac's *Contes drolatiques*, there was a package of cigarettes, and some matches.

I cranked up the Victrola and put on a record of the "Hymn to the Sun," from the *Coq d'Or*. It was the most wonderful music in the world. When that was finished I put on a record of Ukulele Ike singing "I Can't Get the One I Want," and it was just as wonderful. Listening happily I went about the business of straightening the bureau-tops, blowing the dust off vigorously, and arranging toilet articles in a sort of pious symmetry. When I brought out the broom and carpet sweeper I realized for the hundredth time how fortunate we were. To the furnishing of our room Terry's mother had contributed a huge pink Oriental rug with a fine delicate pattern and the bloom of silk. It must have been very valuable; old Mrs. Purchase, a lady of culture who had endowed the school with a library and then come along to see that it was taken care of, was always creeping in to study the rug and shake her head, and once we had even found her down on her knees with a bottle of Carbona, cleaning off a spot. Aside from its beauty and its silky warmth to our bare soles, we appreciated it for another reason. As I moved about on it now, making casual swipes with the carpet sweeper, the whole rosy expanse crunched and crepitated gently under my feet, for in its passive way the rug had saved us many minutes of time, and much dull traffic with dustpans.

In the middle of the morning the bell rang again, sounding strange at this unaccustomed hour, but we all knew what it meant, and began getting out our sweaters and galoshes.

"Who wants to see the damned old eclipse, anyway," said Terry again, pulling on the leopard coat. "We'll just stand around freezing for *hours* and *hours.*"

"Well, I prefer it to *Julius Caesar,*" I said. "I certainly prefer it to *physics!*" The truth was that I felt the wildest excitement at the prospect of seeing a total eclipse, but thought it would be naïve to say so.

Nydia and I each borrowed a fur coat from Terry; Marcia had her own coonskin one, made just like a college boy's without any shape at all. Terry borrowed a hat from Nydia and I loaned one to Marcia, and she loaned me an extra sweater and Nydia borrowed my angora mittens. We all wore our galoshes unbuckled because that was the way to wear them, and when we walked down the stairs we jingled like a detachment of cavalry.

Outdoors a procession of station wagons had been commandeered from the parents of day pupils. An air of revelry prevailed, causing the younger children to leap in the air and squeal. I would have liked to leap and squeal myself, but of course I didn't.

Finally, after the usual delay and confusion, we were packed into our appointed places in the station wagons, and the journey began. The world was white with fallen snow, and we looked deep, deep into the bare-boned woods that edged the road. I remember the jovial metallic snack-snack-snack of the tire chains, and the starling chittering of the younger children in the car behind.

Miles away we stopped at the foot of a great bald hill where the view was said to be the best in the region.

"You mean we're going to *climb* the thing?" said Terry. She detested exercise, and her techniques for evading basketball practice were formidable.

"I bet I'll be winded," Nydia murmured with pride. She had been known to smoke as many as seven cigarettes in one day.

We toiled up the broad flank of the hill through deep snow. Our unbuckled galoshes clapped and clattered and caught at the hems of our skirts; snow slopped over the tops of them. Erratic as squirrels, the younger children darted and zigzagged, while the teachers and parents, their overshoes sensibly fastened, forged steadily ahead with the Spartan philosophical gait peculiar to adults on an outing with children.

Luckily the day was fair, though already a strangeness had come into the light, like the light in dreams, and it was bitterly cold. The dome of the hill, when we reached it, was immense—a vast rounded plain. Against the waste of white the scattered groups of people seemed diminished and at the same time sharpened in outline; adjuncts to nature, like the figures in Breughel snow-pieces.

Mr. Muller, the science teacher, had built a fire up there. He and Mr. Ripley, the math teacher, were squatted beside it, smoking pieces of glass. My feelings about Mr. Muller were mixed. Every December for the last three years I had taken the part of Mary in the school Nativity play, and Mr. Muller was always Joseph. Three times he had led me across the wilderness of the assembly room, in

front of the thrilling, rustling audience, to the door of
the secretary's office where we were denied shelter for the
night, and from there up the broad staircase to Bethlehem
on the landing. Here we disappeared for a moment and
then, curtains parting, I was seen beside the manger wearing a gildled buckram halo and gazing earnestly into a
150-watt Mazda bulb. The world would be green for an
hour afterward, and I remember feelings of exaltation and
gratified ego; but somehow I could not help wishing that
somebody else, not Mr. Muller, might have been Joseph.

He and Mr. Ripley handed out the pieces of blackened
glass and strips of exposed negative. We had been warned
not to look at the sun without one of these protections,
and now, holding up my sooty glass, I took my first look.

The sun was in crescent, an imitation of the moon, a
humble step down from power. It looked no different from
the several partial eclipses I had seen in my life, and I
was disappointed.

The younger children played in the snow and screamed.
Nydia giggled with Tom Frank, one of our classmates, and
Marcia, in low tones, was giving advice to Hank McCurdy,
another classmate. She loved to give advice, especially to
boys. Terry paced to and fro, lost in her own thoughts.

The light was weakening and weakening and the cold
growing: a deathly cold. We began to stamp and beat our
hands together, and when a thermos of hot cocoa was
produced there were cheers.

"Why couldn't it be coffee!" murmured sophisticated
Marcia.

Whenever I looked at the sun through the black glass
it had grown narrowed; and finally it was little more than a
sickle of reddish light. Then less. Less . . . Still less.

And now the miracle took place. I dropped my glass.
Across the snow, suddenly, ran streamers of shadow and
iridescent light, wavering bands turning and turning in
an unimaginable wheel of rays. What was happening?
There was a startling impression of swiftness, as if something—someone?—hastened forward to a climax. The sky

darkened abruptly. A great still coldness dropped onto the world and all around its edge there was a band of orange light, like the instant before sunrise on all the horizons of the earth at once.

"Look up! Look, look, look," whispered Terry.

In the deep sky where there had been a sun, we saw a ring of white silver; a smoking ring, and all the smokes were silver, too; gauzy, fuming, curling, unbelievable. And who had ever seen the sky this color! Not in earliest morning nor at twilight, never before had we seen or dreamed this strange immortal blue in which a few large stars now sparkled as though for the first time of all.

At some point I glanced for an instant at those nearest me. I had never seen before, nor have I since, the expression of total awe on the faces of a crowd; all turned upward, arrested, self-forgotten, like the faces of revelation in old religious paintings.

There were tears on Terry's cheeks, I remember, and Carla Cudlipp, a fat pragmatical girl, was on her knees in the snow in an attitude of prayer. Even Miss Lagrange, a battle axe if ever one lived, was trembling all over like a frightened child.

But I watched them for no longer than a second; it was more important to watch, to try to memorize, that marvelous smoking circle of light, where all too soon the blinding edge of crescent appeared and one could look no longer, and had no wish to look.

We were quiet going down the hill again; even the younger children were quiet: "Gosh," said Marcia, and sighed. It seemed as suitable a comment as any.

All of us were frozen with cold, subdued, spotted with soot. The world once more was muted in the queer dreamlight. Nothing seemed familiar.

"But suppose you'd never seen the sun set in your life," said Nydia suddenly. "Suppose you'd never seen a rainbow. It would be the same thing; you'd be just as—as dumbfounded. You know, you'd get this same terrific kick out of it. I mean it's not a phenomenon or God or anything, it's just that the moon gets in front of the sun once in a while; just a natural thing. It's only that you hardly ever get to *see* it."

"Yes, but gosh, when you do see it, it makes everything else seem more wonderful," I said. "It's as though they let you in on the secret for a minute or two; I mean it's sort of as though they let you remember how it all works and how *wonderful* it is!"

But it was beyond my powers to express what it meant. I fell silent, trying to recapture in memory the exact impression, the exact sensation, of that instant when the universe had seemed to open like a door before me, or my own eyes to open and behold for the first time.

We felt that we had been away for months. Everything in our room, when we returned, looked childish, trivial, and cheap.

Marcia hurled her coat on the bed, smoothed her sweater down on her hips, sighed.

"I know! Let's have a snack before lunch," she said, brightening. Then she went to the cabinet and brought out the box of crackers and the marshmallow whip, settling comfortably on her bed with them, spreading the crackers with a lavish hand. She held one out to me. I had not realized I was so hungry, and went on eating when the others had stopped, although I knew it would be a matter of minutes until the lunch bell rang.

Nydia went to the mirror and refreshed herself at her own reflection for a while, then she turned to the Victrola, cranked it up, and put on a record called "Brown Eyes Why Are You Blue?" Recklessly, she reached in the cabinet and brought out a cigarette, lighted it, and began dancing slowly with her eyes closed, as if asleep. She had learned, by diligent application, to hold the smoke in her mouth for a long time and then let it out gradually through her nostrils, and she did this now. She looked very worldly. I sat watching her as I crunched steadily through the box of soda crackers.

Terry, oblivious of all, was writing yet another somber letter to her Jack—(she had written three the day before)—and Marcia was polishing her nails with a buffer; the pearl ring she had been given on her sixteenth birthday gleamed and winked rhythmically.

There was a noise in the hall outside our room and Nydia's blue eyes flew open. She stubbed out the cigarette on the sole of her shoe, tossed it into the waste basket, and stood a moment listening, holding her breath and fanning away the smoke. Then she laughed.

"Come on, Lib," she said to me, holding out her hands. "Let's dance, you need the practice, you're still terrible. I'll lead."

Humbly and doggedly I did my best to follow. Terry looked up and smiled at us vaguely from her remote place. Marcia watched my feet. "Try not to trudge," she said.

Little by little we were curing ourselves of wonder, and the universe shrank back to its small customary size.

SEVENTEEN

by William Saroyan

SAM WOLINSKY was seventeen, and a month had passed since he had begun to shave; now he was in love. And he wanted to do something. A feeling of violence was in him, and he was thinking of himself as something enormous in the world. He felt drunk with strength that had accumulated from the first moment of his life to the moment he was now living, and he felt almost insane because of the strength. Death was nothing. It could not matter if he died; feeling as he did, it could not matter. All that mattered was this moment, Wolinsky in love, alive, walking down Ventura Avenue, in America, Wolinsky of the universe, the crazy Polak with the broken nose.

Everything was small, beneath his enormity, and he was seeking something to do, some cruelty; it was godly to be cruel, to hurt, even to destroy. It was proper to mock soft feelings in man, to stand by, laughing at the pettiness of man. There was no sacred thing in the world. He knew; he was certain; everything was made in a profane way, and there was no sense in trying to change ugly things into lovely things, no use being dishonest.

He was in love and there was no girl. He was in love with female whiteness, the swelling of female parts, the curve of back, the soft cohesion of limbs uniting in wholeness, hair, smile or strong frown as of passion, female motion, woman, but mostly the idea of woman. He felt no tenderness, and he had no wish to imitate the moving-picture males, touching the females. That was fake. It was fraudulence. They were trying to keep people unaware of the truth, making it a soft event, a thing of no strength. They were trying to hide the animal drive in man, the lust to function violently, but they couldn't fool him, Wolinsky. And the love songs: all rot. And the male weeping: disgusting. A man had to be alone, something by himself. Always a man had to be above occurrences; he had to stand up and laugh at the way things happened, the inevitable way.

He was a slight boy with sad Polish eyes, small for his age, fidgety, a lover of books, loud in conversation. At thirteen he began to read books that were said to be evil, books with thoughts in them that were said to be vile, about women, Schopenhauer, and reading these books he began to expand, growing large inwardly. He became disdainful, aloof, mocking, and he made impolite remarks to his school-teachers, shocking them, seeking trouble everywhere, a chance to quarrel, to be angry, a chance not to be passive and indifferent and half asleep about life. It was all excessive nervousness, and it came partly from the books he read and partly from himself, the way he was, inevitably, insane with life.

Nevertheless, there was a strange tenderness in him that he could never efface, and every now and then he would stare at himself in a mirror and see the tenderness in his eyes. It would make him frantic. He didn't want to be that way. He didn't want to be weak like other people. He was proud because he hadn't once cried in ten years. And he knew there had been many occasions for him to cry. The time he struck his father and felt inwardly unclean. It was never for himself that he had wanted to cry; for others, for hurting something in them, but he had always made himself laugh.

All his life he had wanted to be fully alive, physically, violently, and now he was beginning to feel what it was like. The feeling of vastness in him, the sense of unlimited strength, the mockery in his heart for sacred things, the ribaldry that he felt in regard to love. Love? He knew all about that nonsense. He had read an article in *The Haldeman-Julius Monthly* about love, and he knew. Love was purely physical; all the rest was imaginary, stupid, fake.

Strength accumulated in man and had to be released. It was not personal; it was abstract, universal. One woman was the same as another; it was the function, the act that was inevitable.

Any man who got soft inside about the lust that was in him was a fool. Any man who felt shame was a fool. Man was thus, the chemical situation was thus, there was nothing else to it. And the married women in church, singing, it was laughable: Freud said they were merely doing in a very subtle way what they dared not even think of doing: fornicating. Pathetic and amusing, pious ladies committing spiritual adultery in church, on Sunday. It was a fine thing to know, to laugh about. There was at least some godliness in being truthful, even if a man had to be a little vulgar.

There was no girl. All his life something had kept him apart. He had felt love for certain girls in school, but something had kept him apart from them. First it was a feeling that he was unworthy. This feeling was mingled with a consciousness of prejudice against his race. To the others he was a Polak, nothing, nobody. Then it was timidity, then pride, and ever since it had remained pride. He could walk alone. He did not need to humiliate himself by asking a girl to be interested in him, wanting her body and all the rest of it. The soul. The part that really didn't exist, according to science and *The Haldeman-Julius Monthly*, but somehow seemed always to be there in girls. The way they looked at things, the way they came out of their eyes, dancing or being naked or running violently, or weeping. He had seen the girls emerging from their eyes, and it had been very subtle, but he had understood the innate structure of each girl, the specific manner of motion. And always he had preferred the ones who had left themselves violently.

He was a bit mad; he was certain of it, but it never worried him and he was never ashamed. It was out of the accumulated strength in him that his madness emerged in his conduct. One day, walking, he struck a telephone post with his fist, and the knuckles bled and his fist became swollen with pain, but he was not ashamed. He had been walking along, feeling expansive and large, and suddenly he had done it, not thinking about it one way or another. That was all: something to do, some cruelty. The post might have been a man, or life, or God, the idea of these things. It might have been all men, man. He had simply struck. A hurt fist was nothing. Inside he had felt exhilarated. He had laughed, shaking his hand with the pain, laughing about it.

And his fights with other boys; they had always refreshed him. The least little thing would make him fight, and he didn't care how large a boy might be. All he wanted was to function with strength, violently, to let himself out. They had broken his nose twice, but he hadn't felt sorry. He was only a Polak. Physically, he was small. His features were hardly masculine. He knew all about these things. But inside; nobody could say that he wasn't a man. He had taken pains to prove it. All his life he had taken pains to be stronger, braver than his fellows. He had been one of the first boys to begin smoking cigarettes at Longfellow School. He had been thirteen at the time. All the same, there was this old tenderness in him, and it was inexplicable.

It was Sunday afternoon, September, and he was walking down Ventura Avenue, on his way to town. It was thick in him, the old lust, only in a new way: something besides fighting, striking things, a maddening sexual feeling, a desire for the universe, a desire to attack and violate it, to make his reality specific, to establish his presence on earth. He felt no need to apologize for the bawdy feeling that was in him. It was not his fault. He hadn't established the basis of the universe, the manner of life, the method of remaining sane.

He met many friends in Court House Park where the afternoon band concert was being held, boys who feared and respected him, but secretly disliked him. He knew they did not like him. He had no friends. He was alone. He disliked the town; it was small and petty, full of the weaknesses of man. He felt himself to be a stranger in the place. And these boys who greeted him were merely the boys with whom he had grown up. They were in the park because of the girls, the girls with whom they had grown up. What they were doing was pathetic. Woman to him was more than the girls of his time. She was something primarily evil, something vast, eternal and ungiggling. All these girls were full of giggles. They giggled every time a boy looked at them. He walked about in the park, listening to the music in the summer air, watching the boys trying to make the girls, feeling the lust growing in him; then he left the park and began to walk toward Chinatown.

There were some whores over there; he heard the music fading away, the town dwindling away from his mind with the music. He crossed the Southern Pacific tracks on Tulare Street, and began to walk among the Mexicans and Hindus and Chinese of Chinatown. The place was filthy with a filth that was man's, but he had never been squeamish. The player-piano of the Lyceum Theatre was making a nervous racket, and a crowd of Mexicans and Negroes was standing in front of the theatre, eating peanuts and sunflower seeds, talking loudly. He saw one Mexican face that somehow angered him, the face itself, and for a moment he wanted to start a fight. It was strange: something unclean in man that had found expression in the face, and he wanted to object to the face physically. And the musical, sing-song Mexican talk; it annoyed him. It was too soft and effortless, not hard and solid like English, not precise. He wondered where the women could be, and he walked up a block to F Street. On the corner, a poolroom full of Chinese and Mexicans, much smoke, and no sight of female face or figure.

He began to look up second-story windows, seeking some sign of professional evil. He saw red flower pots on window sills with sickly geranium plants growing out of them, and suddenly he began to feel that he was going around like a dog in heat. It made him sick to have such a feeling about himself, and yet he did not want to evade the truth. It was something like that, what he was doing.

There was something of the low animal in it, and he hadn't had such a feeling before.

He wanted to be honest. He had come over to Chinatown to have a woman. He hadn't had the thought in his mind in a secretive way; it hadn't been in the background of his mind in the form of a vague possibility. It had been specific, outright. He would never be able to maintain his belief in himself if he did not go through with it. He began to look around for certain doorways, passageways leading to such places, small hotels. Nothing looked evil. Nothing seemed vast and universal and strong. The doorways of small hotels were exactly like other doorways. It was incredible. He wasn't seeking something pathetic. He wanted genuine evil, clean and large and bawdy. And all that he saw was narrowness and uncleanliness, and it all reflected the dirt and weakness of man, his essential cheapness. He wanted to fight somebody, but recognized the wish as a subtle evasion and refused to entertain the thought.

It was not a question of doing something with his fists; it was a question of finding out definitely about evil, whether or not it was in man to be really strong, or if it was essential for him to be something eternally small and maudlin. He felt this truth cleanly, accurately.

Scrambling up the stairs of a small hotel, he remembered himself suddenly scrambling up the stairs of a small hotel in Chinatown and he remembered how suddenly, how secretively, he had turned into the passageway.

He stood in the hallway of the hotel, looking about, absorbing the filthiness of the place, not the mere physical filthiness, the rotten odour, the ugliness of the walls, the low ceiling, but the symbolic filthiness of the hotel, the whole idea of it. There was a table in a corner with a small handbell on it, and a sign on the wall, *please ring bell*. He touched the bell and heard it ring, losing his breath. Waiting impatiently, dismissing a wish to run down the stairs and escape, he began to notice that there was no laughter, nothing of the universal about what was going on.

He heard walking in the hall, soft slippers shuffling over

soft carpet, and the sound was pathetic to him. Some common human being was moving toward him; that was all. He heard no sound of strong, godly evil, no laughter. And suddenly he was facing a small woman of fifty with hair on her upper lip, a white hag, and he was looking into her unclean eyes; no evil—filthiness.

He wanted to speak but could not. "I want," he began to say, then gulped and felt ashamed of himself. Then he wished to efface this woman from the earth, to have her politely out of his way, out of all life: her dirt, the rot of her age. Then he did what he believed to be a cowardly thing, the most cowardly thing he had ever done. He smiled. He permitted himself to smile, when as a matter of fact he did not wish to smile at all, when as a matter of fact he wished even to destroy the very idea of this person standing before him, and he knew that his smile must be weak and fake and pathetic.

The smile told what he wanted. "Follow me, honey," said the woman, leading him down the hall. Honey? he thought. From this hag? This sort of weakness and fraudulence, and from this sort of person?

The old woman opened the door of a room, and he went in and sat down. "I'll send a girl right over," said the old woman, going away.

Then he saw himself from away up in the firmament sitting pathetically in a small room, smoking a cigarette, feeling unclean, dirty in every moment of his life, from the first moment to this moment, but refusing to get up and go away, wanting to know, one way or another, strength or weakness, laughter or no laughter.

A half hour later, a mere half hour, he was going down the stairs, remembering all the rotten details, the face, the hands, the body, the way it happened. And the ghastly silence as of death, the absence of strength, the impossibility of laughter, the true ugliness of it.

He fled from Chinatown, delirious with anger and shock and horror. He saw the earth flat and drab, cheap and pointless, and what was worse he saw himself as he was, small, the size of a small man, and cheap and pointless and drab and ungodly, and everything despicable. He wanted to laugh at himself but could not. He wanted to laugh at the whole world, the fraudulence of all things that had life and motion, but could not. He began to walk in the city, not knowing which way to go, not understanding why he was there at all, walking, dreading the thought of ever again going home, and all that he could think of was the ghastly filthiness of truth even, the everlasting pettiness of man, the whole falsity of humanity.

He walked a long while, and at last he went home, entering his father's house. And when he was asked to eat, he said that he was not hungry, and he went to his room and took a book and tried to read. The words were on the pages as evasions, like everything else. He closed the book and tried just sitting and not thinking, but it was impossible.

He could not get over the feeling of the cheapness of the whole thing, the absence of strength, the absence of dignity, the impossibility of laughter.

His mother, worrying, standing at the door of his room, heard him crying. At first she could not believe it, but afterwards she knew that it was real crying, like her own crying sometimes, and she went to the boy's father. "He is in there alone, crying," she said to her husband. "Sammy, our boy, is crying, papa. Sammy. Please go to him, papa. I am afraid. Please see why he is crying." And the poor woman began herself to cry. It made her very happy to cry over her son crying. It made her feel that at last he was like all of them, small and pathetic, a real baby, her boy, and she kept on repeating, "Papa, Sammy is crying; he is crying, papa."

A SUMMER'S READING

by Bernard Malamud

GEORGE STOYONOVICH was a neighborhood boy who had
quit high school on an impulse when he was sixteen, run
out of patience, and though he was ashamed everytime
he went looking for a job, when people asked him if he
had finished and he had to say no, he never went back to
school. This summer was a hard time for jobs and he had
none. Having so much time on his hands, George thought
of going to summer school, but the kids in his classes
would be too young. He also considered registering in a
night high school, only he didn't like the idea of the teachers always telling him what to do. He felt they had not
respected him. The result was he stayed off the streets and
in his room most of the day. He was close to twenty and
had needs with the neighborhood girls, but no money to
spend, and he couldn't get more than an occasional few
cents because his father was poor, and his sister Sophie,
who resembled George, a tall bony girl of twenty-three,
earned very little and what she had she kept for herself.
Their mother was dead, and Sophie had to take care of
the house.

Very early in the morning George's father got up to go
to work in a fish market. Sophie left about eight for her
long ride in the subway to a cafeteria in the Bronx. George
had his coffee by himself, then hung around in the house.
When the house, a five-room railroad flat above a butcher
store, got on his nerves he cleaned it up—mopped the floors
with a wet mop and put things away. But most of the time
he sat in his room. In the afternoons he listened to the
ball game. Otherwise he had a couple of old copies of the

World Almanac he had bought long ago, and he liked to read in them and also the magazines and newspapers that Sophie brought home, that had been left on the tables in the cafeteria. They were mostly picture magazines about movie stars and sports figures, also usually the *News* and *Mirror*. Sophie herself read whatever fell into her hands, although she sometimes read good books.

She once asked George what he did in his room all day and he said he read a lot too.

"Of what besides what I bring home? Do you ever read any worthwhile books?"

"Some," George answered, although he really didn't. He had tried to read a book or two that Sophie had in the house but found he was in no mood for them. Lately he couldn't stand made-up stories, they got on his nerves. He wished he had some hobby to work at—as a kid he was good in carpentry, but where could he work at it? Sometimes during the day he went for walks, but mostly he did his walking after the hot sun had gone down and it was cooler in the streets.

In the evening after supper George left the house and wandered in the neighborhood. During the sultry days some of the storekeepers and their wives sat in chairs on the thick, broken sidewalks in front of their shops, fanning themselves, and George walked past them and the guys hanging out on the candy store corner. A couple of them he had known his whole life, but nobody recognized each other. He had no place special to go, but generally, saving it till the last, he left the neighborhood and walked for blocks till he came to a darkly lit little park with benches and trees and an iron railing, giving it a feeling of privacy. He sat on a bench here, watching the leafy trees and the flowers blooming on the inside of the railing, thinking of a better life for himself. He thought of the jobs he had had since he had quit school—delivery boy, stock clerk, runner, lately working in a factory—and he was dissatisfied with all of them. He felt he would someday like to have a good job and live in a private house with a porch, on a street with trees. He wanted to have some dough in his

pocket to buy things with, and a girl to go with, so as not
to be so lonely, especially on Saturday nights. He wanted
people to like and respect him. He thought about these
things often but mostly when he was alone at night.
Around midnight he got up and drifted back to his hot
and stony neighborhood.

One time while on his walk George met Mr. Cattanzara
coming home very late from work. He wondered if he was
drunk but then could tell he wasn't. Mr. Cattanzara, a
stocky, bald-headed man who worked in a change booth
on an IRT station, lived on the next block after George's,
above a shoe repair store. Nights, during the hot weather,
he sat on his stoop in an undershirt, reading the *New York
Times* in the light of the shoemaker's window. He read it
from the first page to the last, then went up to sleep. And
all the time he was reading the paper, his wife, a fat
woman with a white face, leaned out of the window,
gazing into the street, her thick white arms folded under
her loose breast, on the window ledge.

Once in a while Mr. Cattanzara came home drunk, but
it was a quiet drunk. He never made any trouble, only
walked stiffly up the street and slowly climbed the stairs
into the hall. Though drunk, he looked the same as always,
except for his tight walk, the quietness, and that his eyes
were wet. George liked Mr. Cattanzara because he remembered him giving him nickels to buy lemon ice with when
he was a squirt. Mr. Cattanzara was a different type than
those in the neighborhood. He asked different questions
than the others when he met you, and he seemed to know
what went on in all the newspapers. He read them, as his
fat sick wife watched from the window.

"What are you doing with yourself this summer,
George?" Mr. Cattanzara asked. "I see you walkin' around
at nights."

George felt embarrassed. "I like to walk."

"What are you doin' in the day now?"

"Nothing much just right now. I'm waiting for a job."
Since it shamed him to admit he wasn't working, George

said, "I'm staying home—but I'm reading a lot to pick up my education."

Mr. Cattanzara looked interested. He mopped his hot face with a red handkerchief.

"What are you readin'?"

George hesitated, then said, "I got a list of books in the library once, and now I'm gonna read them this summer." He felt strange and a little unhappy saying this, but he wanted Mr. Cattanzara to respect him.

"How many books are there on it?"

"I never counted them. Maybe around a hundred."

Mr. Cattanzara whistled through his teeth.

"I figure if I did that," George went on earnestly, "it would help me in my education. I don't mean the kind they give you in high school. I want to know different things than they learn there, if you know what I mean."

The change maker nodded. "Still and all, one hundred books is a pretty big load for one summer."

"It might take longer."

"After you're finished with some, maybe you and I can shoot the breeze about them?" said Mr. Cattanzara.

"When I'm finished," George answered.

Mr. Cattanzara went home and George continued on his walk. After that, though he had the urge to, George did nothing different from usual. He still took his walks at night, ending up in the little park. But one evening the shoemaker on the next block stopped George to say he was a good boy, and George figured that Mr. Cattanzara had told him all about the books he was reading. From the shoemaker it must have gone down the street, because George saw a couple of people smiling kindly at him, though nobody spoke to him personally. He felt a little better around the neighborhood and liked it more, though not so much he would want to live in it forever. He had never exactly disliked the people in it, yet he had never liked them very much either. It was the fault of the neighborhood. To his surprise, George found out that his father and Sophie knew about his reading too. His father was too shy to say anything about it—he was never much of a talker in his whole life—but Sophie was softer to George, and she showed him in other ways she was proud of him.

As the summer went on George felt in a good mood about things. He cleaned the house every day, as a favor to Sophie, and he enjoyed the ball games more. Sophie gave him a buck a week allowance, and though it still wasn't enough and he had to use it carefully, it was a helluva lot better than just having two bits now and then. What he bought with the money—cigarettes mostly, an occasional beer or movie ticket—he got a big kick out of. Life wasn't so bad if you knew how to appreciate it. Occasionally he bought a paperback book from the news-stand, but he never got around to reading it, though he was glad to have a couple of books in his room. But he read thoroughly Sophie's magazines and newspapers. And at night was the most enjoyable time, because when he passed the store-keepers sitting outside their stores, he could tell they regarded him highly. He walked erect, and though he did not say much to them, or they to him, he could feel approval on all sides. A couple of nights he felt so good that he skipped the park at the end of the evening. He just wandered in the neighborhood, where people had known him from the time he was a kid playing punchball whenever there was a game of it going; he wandered there, then came home and got undressed for bed, feeling fine.

For a few weeks he had talked only once with Mr. Cattanzara, and though the change maker had said nothing more about the books, asked no questions, his silence made George a little uneasy. For a while George didn't pass in front of Mr. Cattanzara's house anymore, until one night, forgetting himself, he approached it from a different direction than he usually did when he did. It was already past midnight. The street, except for one or two people, was deserted, and George was surprised when he saw Mr. Cattanzara still reading his newspaper by the light of the street lamp overhead. His impulse was to stop at the stoop and talk to him. He wasn't sure what he wanted to say, though he felt the words would come when he began to talk; but the more he thought about it, the more the idea scared him, and he decided he'd better not. He even considered beating it home by another street, but he was too near Mr. Cattanzara, and the change maker might see him as he ran, and get annoyed. So George unobtrusively crossed the street, trying to make it seem as if he had to look in a store window on the other side, which he did, and then went on, uncomfortable at what he was doing. He feared Mr. Cattanzara would glance up from his paper and call him a dirty rat for walking on the other side of the street, but all he did was sit there, sweating through his undershirt, his bald head shining in the dim light as he read his *Times*, and upstairs his fat wife leaned out of the window, seeming to read the paper along with him. George thought she would spy him and yell out to Mr. Cattanzara, but she never moved her eyes off her husband.

George made up his mind to stay away from the change maker until he had got some of his softback books read, but when he started them and saw they were mostly story books, he lost his interest and didn't bother to finish them. He lost his interest in reading other things too. Sophie's magazines and newspapers went unread. She saw them piling up on a chair in his room and asked why he was no longer looking at them, and George told her it was because of all the other reading he had to do. Sophie said she had guessed that was it. So for most of the day, George had the radio on, turning to music when he was sick of the human voice. He kept the house fairly neat, and Sophie said nothing on the days when he neglected it. She was still kind and gave him his extra buck, though things weren't so good for him as they had been before.

But they were good enough, considering. Also his night walks invariably picked him up, no matter how bad the day was. Then one night George saw Mr. Cattanzara coming down the street toward him. George was about to turn and run but he recognized from Mr. Cattanzara's walk that he was drunk, and if so, probably he would not even bother to notice him. So George kept on walking straight ahead until he came abreast of Mr. Cattanzara and though he felt wound up enough to pop into the sky, he was not surprised when Mr. Cattanzara passed him without a word, walking slowly, his face and body stiff. George drew a breath in relief at his narrow escape, when he heard his name called, and there stood Mr. Cattanzara at his elbow, smelling like the inside of a beer barrel. His eyes were sad as he gazed at George, and George felt so intensely uncomfortable he was tempted to shove the drunk aside and continue on his walk.

But he couldn't act that way to him, and, besides, Mr. Cattanzara took a nickel out of his pants pocket and handed it to him.

"Go buy yourself a lemon ice, Georgie."

"It's not that time anymore, Mr. Cattanzara," George said, "I am a big guy now."

"No, you ain't," said Mr. Cattanzara, to which George made no reply he could think of.

"How are all your books comin' along now?" Mr. Cattanzara asked. Though he tried to stand steady, he swayed a little.

"Fine, I guess," said George, feeling the red crawling up his face.

"You ain't sure?" The change maker smiled slyly, a way George had never seen him smile.

"Sure I'm sure. They're fine."

Though his head swayed in little arcs, Mr. Cattanzara's eyes were steady. He had small blue eyes which could hurt if you looked at them too long.

"George," he said, "name me one book on that list that you read this summer, and I will drink to your health."

"I don't want anybody drinking to me."

"Name me one so I can ask you a question on it. Who can tell, if it's a good book maybe I might wanna read it myself."

George knew he looked passable on the outside, but inside he was crumbling apart.

Unable to reply, he shut his eyes, but when—years later —he opened them, he saw that Mr. Cattanzara had, out of pity, gone away, but in his ears he still heard the words he had said when he left: "George, don't do what I did."

The next night he was afraid to leave his room, and though Sophie argued with him he wouldn't open the door.

"What are you doing in there?" she asked.

"Nothing."

"Aren't you reading?"

"No."

She was silent a minute, then asked, "Where do you keep the books you read? I never see any in your room outside of a few cheap trashy ones."

He wouldn't tell her.

"In that case you're not worth a buck of my hard-earned money. Why should I break my back for you? Go on out, you bum, and get a job."

He stayed in his room for almost a week, except to sneak into the kitchen when nobody was home. Sophie railed at him, then begged him to come out, and his old father wept, but George wouldn't budge, though the weather was terrible and his small room stifling. He found it very hard to breathe, each breath was like drawing a flame into his lungs.

One night, unable to stand the heat anymore, he burst into the street at one A.M., a shadow of himself. He hoped to sneak to the park without being seen, but there were people all over the block, wilted and listless, waiting for a breeze. George lowered his eyes and walked, in disgrace, away from them, but before long he discovered they were still friendly to him. He figured Mr. Cattanzara hadn't told on him. Maybe when he woke up out of his drunk the next morning, he had forgotten all about meeting George. George felt his confidence slowly come back to him.

That same night a man on a street corner asked him if it was true that he had finished reading so many books, and George admitted he had. The man said it was a wonderful thing for a boy his age to read so much.

"Yeah," George said, but he felt relieved. He hoped nobody would mention the books anymore, and when, after a couple of days, he accidentally met Mr. Cattanzara again, *he* didn't, though George had the idea he was the one who had started the rumor that he had finished all the books.

One evening in the fall, George ran out of his house to the library, where he hadn't been in years. There were books all over the place, wherever he looked, and though he was struggling to control an inward trembling, he easily counted off a hundred, then sat down at a table to read.

SUCKER

by Carson McCullers

IT WAS ALWAYS like I had a room to myself. Sucker slept in my bed with me but that didn't interfere with anything. The room was mine and I used it as I wanted to. Once I remember sawing a trap door in the floor. Last year when I was a sophomore in high school I tacked on my wall some pictures of girls from magazines and one of them was just in her underwear. My mother never bothered me because she had the younger kids to look after. And Sucker thought anything I did was always swell.

Whenever I would bring any of my friends back to my room all I had to do was just glance once at Sucker and he would get up from whatever he was busy with and maybe half smile at me, and leave without saying a word. He never brought kids back there. He's twelve, four years younger than I am, and he always knew without me even telling him that I didn't want kids that age meddling with my things.

Half the time I used to forget that Sucker isn't my brother. He's my first cousin but practically ever since I remember he's been in our family. You see his folks were killed in a wreck when he was a baby. To me and my kid sisters he was like our brother.

Sucker used to always remember and believe every word I said. That's how he got his nick-name. Once a couple of years ago I told him that if he'd jump off our garage with an umbrella it would act as a parachute and he wouldn't fall hard. He did it and busted his knee. That's just one instance. And the funny thing was that no matter how many times he got fooled he would still believe me.

Not that he was dumb in other ways—it was just the way he acted with me. He would look at everything I did and quietly take it in.

There is one thing I have learned, but it makes me feel guilty and is hard to figure out. If a person admires you a lot you despise him and don't care—and it is the person who doesn't notice you that you are apt to admire. This is not easy to realize. Maybelle Watts, this senior at school, acted like she was the Queen of Sheba and even humiliated me. Yet at this same time I would have done anything in the world to get her attentions. All I could think about day and night was Maybelle until I was nearly crazy. When Sucker was a little kid and on up until the time he was twelve I guess I treated him as bad as Maybelle did me.

Now that Sucker has changed so much it is a little hard to remember him as he used to be. I never imagined anything would suddenly happen that would make us both very different. I never knew that in order to get what has happened straight in my mind I would want to think back on him as he used to be and compare and try to get things settled. If I could have seen ahead maybe I would have acted different.

I never noticed him much or thought about him and when you consider how long we have had the same room together it is funny the few things I remember. He used to talk to himself a lot when he'd think he was alone—all about him fighting gangsters and being on ranches and that sort of kids' stuff. He'd get in the bathroom and stay as long as an hour and sometimes his voice would go up high and excited and you could hear him all over the house. Usually, though, he was very quiet. He didn't have many boys in the neighborhood to buddy with and his face had the look of a kid who is watching a game and waiting to be asked to play. He didn't mind wearing the sweaters and coats that I outgrew, even if the sleeves did flop down too big and make his wrists look as thin and white as a little girl's. That is how I remember him—getting a little bigger every year but still being the same. That was

Sucker up until a few months ago when all this trouble began.

Maybelle was somehow mixed up in what happened so I guess I ought to start with her. Until I knew her I hadn't given much time to girls. Last fall she sat next to me in General Science class and that was when I first began to notice her. Her hair is the brightest yellow I ever saw and occasionally she will wear it set into curls with some sort of gluey stuff. Her fingernails are pointed and manicured and painted a shiny red. All during class I used to watch Maybelle, nearly all the time except when I thought she was going to look my way or when the teacher called on me. I couldn't keep my eyes off her hands, for one thing. They are very little and white except for that red stuff, and when she would turn the pages of her book she always licked her thumb and held out her little finger and turned very slowly. It is impossible to describe Maybelle. All the boys are crazy about her but she didn't even notice me. For one thing she's almost two years older than I am. Between periods I used to try and pass very close to her in the halls but she would hardly ever smile at me. All I could do was sit and look at her in class—and sometimes it was like the whole room could hear my heart beating and I wanted to holler or light out and run for Hell.

At night, in bed, I would imagine about Maybelle. Often this would keep me from sleeping until as late as one or two o'clock. Sometimes Sucker would wake up and ask me why I couldn't get settled and I'd tell him to hush his mouth. I suppose I was mean to him lots of times. I guess I wanted to ignore somebody like Maybelle did me. You could always tell by Sucker's face when his feelings were hurt. I don't remember all the ugly remarks I must have made because even when I was saying them my mind was on Maybelle.

That went on for nearly three months and then somehow she began to change. In the halls she would speak to me and every morning she copied my homework. At lunch time once I danced with her in the gym. One afternoon I got up nerve and went around to her house with a carton of cigarettes. I knew she smoked in the girls' basement and sometimes outside of school—and I didn't want to take her candy because I think that's been run into the ground. She was very nice and it seemed to me everything was going to change.

It was that night when this trouble really started. I had come into my room late and Sucker was already asleep. I felt too happy and keyed up to get in a comfortable position and I was awake thinking about Maybelle a long time. Then I dreamed about her and it seemed I kissed her. It was a surprise to wake up and see the dark. I lay still and a little while passed before I could come to and understand where I was. The house was quiet and it was a very dark night.

Sucker's voice was a shock to me. "Pete? . . ."

I didn't answer anything or even move.

"You do like me as much as if I was your own brother, don't you Pete?"

I couldn't get over the surprise of everything and it was like this was the real dream instead of the other.

"You have liked me all the time like I was your own brother, haven't you?"

"Sure," I said.

Then I got up for a few minutes. It was cold and I was glad to come back to bed. Sucker hung on to my back. He felt little and warm and I could feel his warm breathing on my shoulder.

"No matter what you did I always knew you liked me."

I was wide awake and my mind seemed mixed up in a strange way. There was this happiness about Maybelle and all that—but at the same time something about Sucker and his voice when he said these things made me take notice. Anyway I guess you understand people better when you are happy than when something is worrying you. It was like I had never really thought about Sucker until then. I felt I had always been mean to him. One night a few weeks before I had heard him crying in the dark. He said he had lost a boy's beebee gun and was scared to let anybody know. He wanted me to tell him what to do. I was sleepy and tried to make him hush and when he wouldn't I kicked at him. That was just one of the things I remembered. It seemed to me he had always been a lonesome kid. I felt bad.

There is something about a dark cold night that makes you feel close to someone you're sleeping with. When you talk together it is like you are the only people awake in the town.

"You're a swell kid, Sucker," I said.

It seemed to me suddenly that I did like him more than anybody else I knew—more than any other boy, more than my sisters, more in a certain way even than Maybelle. I felt good all over and it was like when they play sad music in the movies. I wanted to show Sucker how much I really thought of him and make up for the way I had always treated him.

We talked for a good while that night. His voice was fast and it was like he had been saving up these things to tell me for a long time. He mentioned that he was going to try to build a canoe and that the kids down the block wouldn't let him in on their football team and I don't know what all. I talked some too and it was a good feeling to think of him taking in everything I said so seriously. I even spoke of Maybelle a little, only I made out like it was her who had been running after me all this time. He asked questions about high school and so forth. His voice was excited and he kept on talking fast like he could never get the words out in time. When I went to sleep he was still talking and I could still feel his breathing on my shoulder, warm and close.

During the next couple of weeks I saw a lot of Maybelle. She acted as though she really cared for me a little. Half the time I felt so good I hardly knew what to do with myself.

But I didn't forget about Sucker. There were a lot of old things in my bureau drawer I'd been saving—boxing gloves and Tom Swift books and second-rate fishing tackle. All this I turned over to him. We had some more talks together and it was really like I was knowing him for the first time. When there was a long cut on his cheek I knew he had been monkeying around with this new first razor set of mine, but I didn't say anything. His face seemed different now. He used to look timid and sort of like he was afraid of a whack over the head. That expression was gone. His face, with those wide-open eyes and his ears sticking out and his mouth never quite shut, had the look of a person who is surprised and expecting something swell.

Once I started to point him out to Maybelle and tell her he was my kid brother. It was an afternoon when a murder mystery was on at the movie. I had earned a dollar working for my Dad and I gave Sucker a quarter to go and get candy and so forth. With the rest I took Maybelle. We were sitting near the back and I saw Sucker come in. He began to stare at the screen the minute he stepped past the ticket man and he stumbled down the aisle without noticing where he was going. I started to punch Maybelle but couldn't quite make up my mind. Sucker looked a little silly—walking like a drunk with his eyes glued to the movie. He was wiping his reading glasses on his shirt tail and his knickers flopped down. He went on until he got to the first few rows where the kids usually sit. I never did punch Maybelle. But I got to thinking it was good to have both of them at the movie with the money I earned.

I guess things went on like this for about a month or six weeks. I felt so good I couldn't settle down to study or put my mind on anything. I wanted to be friendly with everybody. There were times when I just had to talk to some person. And usually that would be Sucker. He felt as good as I did. Once he said: "Pete, I am gladder that you are like my brother than anything else in the world."

Then something happened between Maybelle and me. I never have figured out just what it was. Girls like her are hard to understand. She began to act different toward me. At first I wouldn't let myself believe this and tried to think it was just my imagination. She didn't act glad to see me any more. Often she went out riding with this fellow on the football team who owns this yellow roadster. The car was the color of her hair and after school she would ride off with him, laughing and looking into his face. I couldn't think of anything to do about it and she was on my mind all day and night. When I did get a chance to go out with her she was snippy and didn't seem to notice me. This made me feel like something was the matter—I would worry about my shoes clopping too loud on the floor, or the fly of my pants, or the bumps on my chin. Sometimes when Maybelle was around, a devil would get into me and I'd hold my face stiff and call grown men by their last names without the Mister and say rough things. In the night I would wonder what made me do all this until I was too tired for sleep.

At first I was so worried I just forgot about Sucker. Then later he began to get on my nerves. He was always hanging around until I would get back from high school, always looking like he had something to say to me or wanted me to tell him. He made me a magazine rack in his Manual Training class and one week he saved his lunch money and bought me three packs of cigarettes. He couldn't seem to take it in that I had things on my mind and didn't want to fool with him. Every afternoon it would be the same—him in my room with this waiting expression on his face. Then I wouldn't say anything or I'd maybe answer him rough-like and he would finally go on out.

I can't divide that time up and say this happened one day and that the next. For one thing I was so mixed up the weeks just slid along into each other and I felt like Hell and didn't care. Nothing definite was said or done. Maybelle still rode around with this fellow in his yellow roadster and sometimes she would smile at me and sometimes not. Every afternoon I went from one place to another where I thought she would be. Either she would act almost nice and I would begin thinking how things would finally clear up and she would care for me—or else she'd behave so that if she hadn't been a girl I'd have wanted to grab her by that white little neck and choke her. The more ashamed I felt for making a fool of myself the more I ran after her.

Sucker kept getting on my nerves more and more. He would look at me as though he sort of blamed me for something, but at the same time knew that it wouldn't last long. He was growing fast and for some reason began to stutter when he talked. Sometimes he had nightmares or would throw up his breakfast. Mom got him a bottle of cod liver oil.

Then the finish came between Maybelle and me. I met her going to the drug store and asked for a date. When she said no I remarked something sarcastic. She told me she was sick and tired of my being around and that she had never cared a rap about me. She said all that. I just stood there and didn't answer anything. I walked home very slowly.

For several afternoons I stayed in my room by myself. I didn't want to go anywhere or talk to anyone. When Sucker would come in and look at me sort of funny I'd yell at him to get out. I didn't want to think of Maybelle and I sat at my desk reading *Popular Mechanics* or whittling at a toothbrush rack I was making. It seemed to me I was putting that girl out of my mind pretty well.

But you can't help what happens to you at night. That is what made things how they are now.

You see a few nights after Maybelle said those words to me I dreamed about her again. It was like that first time and I was squeezing Sucker's arm so tight I woke him up. He reached for my hand.

"Pete, what's the matter with you?"

All of a sudden I felt so mad my throat choked—at myself and the dream and Maybelle and Sucker and every single person I knew. I remembered all the times Maybelle had humiliated me and everything bad that had ever happened. It seemed to me for a second that nobody would ever like me but a sap like Sucker.

"Why is it we aren't buddies like we were before? Why—?"

"Shut your damn trap!" I threw off the cover and got up and turned on the light. He sat in the middle of the bed, his eyes blinking and scared.

There was something in me and I couldn't help myself. I don't think anybody ever gets that mad but once. Words came without me knowing what they would be. It was only afterward that I could remember each thing I said and see it all in a clear way.

"Why aren't we buddies? Because you're the dumbest slob I ever saw! Nobody cares anything about you! And just because I felt sorry for you sometimes and tried to act decent don't think I give a damn about a dumb-bunny like you!"

If I talked loud or hit him it wouldn't have been so bad. But my voice was slow and like I was very calm. Sucker's mouth was part way open and he looked as though he'd knocked his funny bone. His face was white and sweat came out on his forehead. He wiped it away with the back of his hand and for a minute his arm stayed raised that way as though he was holding something away from him.

"Don't you know a single thing? Haven't you ever been around at all? Why don't you get a girl friend instead of me? What kind of a sissy do you want to grow up to be anyway?"

I didn't know what was coming next. I couldn't help myself or think.

Sucker didn't move. He had on one of my pajama jackets and his neck stuck out skinny and small. His hair was damp on his forehead.

"Why do you always hang around me? Don't you know when you're not wanted?"

Afterward I could remember the change in Sucker's face. Slowly that blank look went away and he closed his mouth. His eyes got narrow and his fists shut. There had never been such a look on him before. It was like every second he was getting older. There was a hard look to his eyes you don't see usually in a kid. A drop of sweat rolled down his chin and he didn't notice. He just sat there with those eyes on me and he didn't speak and his face was hard and didn't move.

"No you don't know when you're not wanted. You're too dumb. Just like your name—a dumb Sucker."

It was like something had busted inside me. I turned off the light and sat down in the chair by the window. My legs were shaking and I was so tired I could have bawled. The room was cold and dark. I sat there for a long time and smoked a squashed cigarette I had saved. Outside the yard was black and quiet. After a while I heard Sucker lie down.

I wasn't mad any more, only tired. It seemed awful to me that I had talked like that to a kid only twelve. I couldn't take it all in. I told myself I would go over to him and try to make it up. But I just sat there in the cold until a long time had passed. I planned how I could straighten it out in the morning. Then, trying not to squeak the springs, I got back in bed.

Sucker was gone when I woke up the next day. And later when I wanted to apologize as I had planned he looked at me in this new hard way so that I couldn't say a word.

All of that was two or three months ago. Since then Sucker has grown faster than any boy I ever saw. He's almost as tall as I am and his bones have gotten heavier and bigger. He won't wear any of my old clothes any more and has bought his first pair of long pants—with some leather suspenders to hold them up. Those are just the changes that are easy to see and put into words.

Our room isn't mine at all any more. He's gotten up this gang of kids and they have a club. When they aren't digging trenches in some vacant lot and fighting they are always in my room. On the door there is some foolishness written in Mercurochrome saying "Woe to the Outsider who Enters" and signed with crossed bones and their secret initials. They have rigged up a radio and every afternoon it blares out music. Once as I was coming in I heard a boy telling something in a low voice about what he saw in the back of his big brother's automobile. I could guess what I didn't hear. *That's what her and my brother do. It's the truth—parked in the car.* For a minute Sucker looked surprised and his face was almost like it used to be. Then he got hard and tough again. "Sure, dumbell. We know all that." They didn't notice me. Sucker began telling them how in two years he was planning to be a trapper in Alaska.

But most of the time Sucker stays by himself. It is worse when we are alone together in the room. He sprawls across the bed in those long corduroy pants with the suspenders and just stares at me with that hard, half sneering look. I fiddle around my desk and can't get settled because of those eyes of his. And the thing is I just have to study because I've gotten three bad cards this term already. If I flunk English I can't graduate next year. I don't want to be a bum and I just have to get my mind on it. I don't care a flip for Maybelle or any particular girl any more and it's only this thing between Sucker and me that is the trouble now. We never speak except when we have to before the family. I don't even want to call him Sucker any more and unless I forget I call him by his real name, Richard. At night I can't study with him in the room and I have to hang around the drug store, smoking and doing nothing, with the fellows who loaf there.

More than anything I want to be easy in my mind again. And I miss the way Sucker and I were for a while in a funny, sad way that before this I never would have believed. But everything is so different that there seems to be nothing I can do to get it right. I've sometimes thought if we could have it out in a big fight that would help. But I can't fight him because he's four years younger. And another thing—sometimes this look in his eyes makes me almost believe that if Sucker could he would kill me.

SNOWFALL IN CHILDHOOD

by Ben Hecht

I GOT OUT OF BED to see what had happened in the night. I was thirteen years old. I had fallen asleep watching the snow falling through the half-frosted window.

But though the snow had promised to keep falling for a long time, perhaps three or four days, on opening my eyes I was full of doubts. Snowstorms usually ended too soon.

While getting out of bed I remembered how, as I was nearly asleep, the night outside the frosted window had seemed to burst into a white jungle. I had dreamed of streets and houses buried in snow.

I hurried barefooted to the window. It was scribbled with a thick frost and I couldn't see through it. The room was cold and through the opened window came the fresh smell of snow like the moist nose of an animal resting on the ledge and breathing into the room.

I knew from the smell and the darkness of the window that snow was falling. I melted a peephole on the glass with my palms. I saw that this time the snow had not fooled me. There it was, still coming down white and silent and too thick for the wind to move, and the streets and houses were almost as I had dreamed. I watched, shivering and happy. Then I dressed, pulling on my clothes as if the house were on fire. I was finished with breakfast and out in the storm two hours before schooltime.

The world had changed. All the houses, fences, and barren trees had new shapes. Everything was round and white and unfamiliar.

I set out through these new streets on a voyage of discovery. The unknown surrounded me. Through the thick falling snow, the trees, houses, and fences looked like ghost shapes that had floated down out of the sky during the night. The morning was without light, but the snowfall hung and swayed like a marvelous lantern over the streets. The snowbanks, already over my head in places, glowed mysteriously.

I was pleased with this new world. It seemed to belong to me more than that other world which lay hidden.

I headed for the school, jumping like a clumsy rabbit in and out of snowbanks. It seemed wrong to spoil the smooth outlines of these snowdrifts and I hoped that nobody else would pass this way after me. In that case the thick falling snow would soon restore the damage. Reassured by this hope I continued on my devastations like some wanton explorer. I began to feel that no one would dare the dangers of my wake. Then, as I became more aware of the noble proportions of this snowstorm, I stopped worrying altogether about the marring of this new and glowing world. Other snows had melted and been shoveled away, but this snow would never disappear. The sun would never shine again and the little Wisconsin town through which I plunged and tumbled to school on this dark storm-filled morning was from now on an arctic land full of danger and adventure.

When eventually, encased in snow, I arrived at the school, I found scores of white-covered figures already there. The girls had taken shelter inside, but the boys stayed in the storm. They jumped in and out of the snowdrifts and tumbled through the deep unbroken white fields in front of the school.

Muffled cries filled the street. Someone had discovered how faraway our voices sounded in the snowfall and this started the screaming. We screamed for ten minutes, delighted with the fact that our voices no longer carried and that the snowstorm had made us nearly dumb.

Tired with two hours of such plunging and rolling, I joined a number of boys who like myself had been busy since dawn and who now stood for the last few minutes before the school bell with half-frozen faces staring at the heavily falling snow as if it were some game they couldn't bear to leave.

When we were finally seated in our grade room, we continued to watch the snowstorm through the windows. The morning had grown darker as we had all hoped it would, and it was necessary to turn on the electric lights in the room. This was almost as thrilling as the pale storm still floating outside the windows.

In this yellow light the school seemed to disappear and in its place a picnic spread around us. The teachers themselves seemed to change. Their eyes kept turning toward the windows and they kept looking at us behind our desks as if we were strangers. We grew excited and even the sound of our lessons—the sentences out of geography and arithmetic books—made us tremble.

Passing through the halls during recess we whispered to one another about the snowstorm, guessing at how deep the snowdrifts must be by this time. We looked nervously at our teachers who stood in the classroom doorways stiff and far removed from our secret whispers about the snow.

I felt sorry for these teachers, particularly for the one who had taught me several years ago when I was in the Fifth Grade. I saw her as I walked by the opened door of her room. She was younger than the other teachers, with two dark braids coiled around her head, a white starched shirtwaist, and soft dark eyes that had always looked kindly at me when I was younger. I saw her now sitting behind her large desk looking over the heads of her class out of the window and paying no attention to the whispers and giggles of her pupils.

As for my own teacher, a tall thin woman with a man's face, by afternoon I had become so happy I could no longer hear what she was saying. I sat looking at the large clock over her head. My feeling on the way to school that it would never be light again and that the snowstorm would keep on forever had increased so that it was something I now knew rather than hoped. My eagerness to get out into the world of wind, gloom, and perpetual snow, kept lifting me out of my seat.

At three o'clock we rushed into the storm. Our screams died as we reached the school entrance. What we saw silenced us. Under the dark sky the street lay piled in an unbroken bank of snow. And above it the snowfall still hung in a thick and moving cloud. Nothing was visible but snow. Everything else had disappeared. Even the sky was gone.

I saw the teachers come out and look around them, frowning. The children of the lower grades stood chattering and frightened near the teachers. I waited until the teacher with the two black braids saw me, and then, paying no attention to her warning, spoken in a gentle voice, I plunged into the storm. I felt brave but slightly regretful that Miss Wheeler could no longer see me as I pushed into the head-high piles of snow and vanished fearlessly into the storm. But I was certain that she was still thinking of me and worrying about my safety. This thought added excitement to the snowstorm.

After an hour I found myself alone. My legs were tired with jumping and my face burned. It had grown darker and the friendliness seemed to have gone out of the storm. The wind bit with a sharper edge and I turned toward my home.

I arrived at the house that now looked like a snowdrift and ploughed my way up to its front door. My heart was beating violently. I stopped to take a last look at the storm. It was hard to leave it. But for the first time in my life an adult logic instructed me. There would be even more snow tomorrow. And in this wind and snow-filled gloom, and even in the marvelously buried street, there was something now unplayful.

I entered the house, calling for something to eat, but as soon as I had taken my coat off and shaken myself clean, I was at the window again. The way this storm was keeping on was hard to believe.

At the table I was too excited to eat. I trembled and was unable to hear what was being said around me. In this room I could feel the night outside and the storm still blowing on my face. It seemed as if I were still in the street. My eyes kept seeing snow and my nose breathing it. The room and the people in it became far away. I left the table, taking a slice of bread and butter with me, and ran upstairs to my own room.

There were a lot of things to do, such as making my leather boots more waterproof by rubbing lard on them, putting my stamp collection in order, sharpening a deer's-foot knife I had recently acquired, winding tape on my new hockey stick, or reading one of the half-dozen new books I had bought with my last birthday money. But none of these activities or even redrawing the plans for the ice-boat on which I was working was possible. I sat in a chair near the window, unable to think. The pale storm in the night seemed to spin like a top, and, keeping the window frost melted with my palms, I sat and watched it snowing for an hour. Then, becoming sleepy, I went to bed. I thought drowsily of how happy Miss Wheeler would be to see me alive on Monday after the way I had rushed into the storm.

There was no seeing through my window when I awoke. The furnace never got going until after seven, and before that hour on a winter's morning the house creaked with cold and the windows were sheeted thick with ice. But I knew as I dressed that the snowfall was over. There was too much wind blowing outside and the breath that came in from the snow-banked window ledge was no longer as fresh as it had been.

It was still dark. The bleak and gusty dawn lay over the snow like a guttering candle. The sky had finished with its snowing but now the wind sent the snowbanks ballooning into the air and the roof tops burst into little snowstorms.

I went outside and explored for ten minutes. When I came back into the house, I needed no warning against going out to play. My skin was almost frozen and the wind was too strong to stand up in. I settled down as a prisoner in front of the fireplace after breakfast, lying on my stomach and turning the pages of a familiar oversized edition of Dante's *Inferno*. It was full of Doré's night-marish pictures.

The house bustled with cooking and cleaning. But these were the dim activities of grownups. I felt alone and took care of the fire to keep it from going out and leaving me to freeze to death. I carried logs all morning from the cellar and lay perspiring and half-scorched on the hearthstone. Every half-hour I went to the window to have a look at the enemy. The sight of the whirling snowbanks and the sound of the brutal wind as it hit against the houses sent me back to the fireplace to scorch myself anew.

In this way I spent the day until late afternoon. It grew dark early. The snow turned leaden. The wind stopped. The dead storm lay in the street and as far as I could see from the window there were no inhabitants in the world. The dark snow was empty. I shivered and went back to the fireplace.

A half-hour later our doorbell rang. Company had arrived for supper. They were the Joneses, who lived in the town of Corliss some eight miles away. They had brought their daughter Anna.

The lights went on in the house. Baked and dizzy with the fire's heat, I joined the two families in the larger parlor. They were talking excitedly about the damage done by the storm. Accounts of store windows blown in, roofs blown off, signs blown down, and wagons abandoned in the drifts were exchanged, and I listened happily. Later, when the talk turned to duller topics, I became aware of Anna.

She was sitting in a corner watching me. She was a blondish girl two years older than I was and she went to high school. I had known her for a long time but had never liked her because she was too calm, never laughing or running, but always looking at people with a sad smile or just a stare as if she had something important on her mind. But now that she was watching me that way, I felt suddenly interested in her. I wondered what she could be thinking of me and what made her smile in that half-sad way at me.

I sat next to her at the table, and after looking at her several times out of the side of my eyes and catching her eyes doing the same thing, my heart started beating faster. I lost interest in eating. I wanted to be alone with her so we could sit and look at each other without the others noticing.

After supper the two families let us go to the hall upstairs, where I kept most of my possessions, without asking us any questions. I found a deck of cards and a cribbage board for a table. Underneath the lapboard our knees touched.

She played cribbage better than I and smiled at me as I kept losing. But I was only half aware of the game. I kept looking at her, unable to talk, and the light pressure of her knees began to make me feel weak. Her face seemed to become brighter and more beautiful as we played. A mist appeared around her eyes and her smile became so close, as if it were moving swiftly toward me, that I began to tremble. I felt ashamed of being so tongue-tied and red-faced, but with a half-frightened, blissful indifference to everything—even Anna—I kept on playing.

We hardly spoke. I grew too nervous to follow the game and I wanted to stop. But I thought if we stopped, we could no longer sit this way with our knees touching. At moments when Anna withdrew her touch, I trembled and waited as if I were hanging from somewhere. When finally her knees returned to their place against mine, I caught my breath and frowned at the cards as if I were completely taken up with them.

As the hour passed, my face began to feel swollen and lopsided and it seemed to me my features had grown ugly beyond words. I tried to distract Anna's attention from this phenomenon by twisting my mouth, screwing up my eyes, and making popping noises with my cheeks as we played. But a new fear arrived to uncenter my attention. I became afraid now that Anna would notice her knees were touching mine and move them away. I began at once pretending a deeper excitement in the game, complaining against my bad luck and denouncing her for cheating. I was determined to keep her interested in the game at any cost, believing that her interest in what we were doing made her unaware of her knees touching mine.

Finally Anna said she was tired of the game. She pushed the cribbage board away. I waited, holding my breath, for her to realize where her knees were and to move them away. I tried not to look at her, but I was so frightened of this happening that I found myself staring at her. She seemed to be paying no attention to me. She was leaning back in her chair and her eyes were half closed. Her face was unsmiling and I felt she was thinking of something. This startled me. My throat filled with questions, but I was so afraid of breaking this hidden embrace of our knees under the lapboard that I said nothing.

The mist seemed to have spread from her eyes to her hair and over the rest of her face. Wherever I looked, this same glow rested around her. I noticed then that her hand was lying on the lapboard. I thought desperately of touching it, but there was something disillusioning in this thought. I watched her fingers begin to tap gently on the board as if she were playing the piano. There was something strange about her hand, as if it did not belong to the way her knees were touching mine or to the mist that rose from her eyes.

The minutes passed in silence and then Anna's mother called her from downstairs.

"I guess they're going home," I said, and Anna nodded. She pressed closer against me, but in my confusion I couldn't figure out whether this was the accidental result of her starting to get out of her chair or on purpose.

"Why don't you ride out with us?" she said. She leaned over the lapboard toward me. "We've got the wagon sleigh and there's plenty of room."

Before I could answer, she had stood up. My knees felt suddenly cold. I slid the lapboard to the floor, ashamed and sad. Anna, without looking back at me, had gone down the stairs. I kept myself from running after her. I was sure she was laughing at me and that she was saying to herself, He's a big fool. He's a big fool.

The Joneses were ready to leave when I came into the parlor. Anna's mother smiled at me.

"Why don't you come and visit us over Sunday?" she said. "There's even more snow in Corliss than here."

"More snow than you can shake a stick at," said another member of the Jones family. They all laughed, and while they were laughing, my mother hustled me off for my wraps. I was to drive away with the Jones family in the sleigh drawn by the two strong horses that stood in front of our house.

I pulled on my leather boots, sweater, and overcoat while the good-bys were being made. I kept trying to catch Anna's attention, but she was apparently unaware that I was in the room. This made me sad, and slowly my eagerness to go to Corliss left me. I wanted instead to go up to my room and slam the door forever on all the Joneses. Anna's gayety, the way she said good-by over and over again and laughed and kissed all the members of my family as if nothing had happened to her, as if she hadn't sat with her eyes closed pressing against my knees in the hallway upstairs, made me almost ill. I felt abandoned and forgotten.

Finally I stood muffled and capped and scowling as my family offered some final instructions for my behavior. I heard nothing of what was said but turned over and over in my mind what I was going to do on the ride and after we got to Corliss. Chiefly I was going to ignore Anna, neither speak to her nor show her by a single look that I knew she was alive.

At this point Anna, having said good-by to everybody several times, seized my arm unexpectedly and whispered against my ear.

"Come, hurry," she said. "We want to get a good place."

Without a word I rushed out of the house, slipping down the snow-caked steps and tumbling headlong into a snow-drift. I scrambled after Anna into the wagon sleigh. It was a low-sided farm wagon placed on wide, heavy wooden runners and piled with warm hay and horse blankets. There was room for only one on the seat. The rest of the Joneses, seven including me, would have to lie in the hay, covered by the robes.

Anna was already in the wagon half-buried in the hay, a blanket over her. She gave me excited orders to brush the snow from my clothes, to cover myself well and not to get out and run alongside the horses when we were going up hill.

"It doesn't help any," she said. "They can pull just the same if you stay in here. And besides, I don't want you to."

The rest of the Joneses came out and crowded into the wagon around us. Anna's father took his place on the driver's seat, assuring my mother, who had come out with a shawl over her head, that there was no danger because the state plow had cleared the road even to way beyond Corliss. I heard my mother ask where I was. Mrs. Jones answered that I was buried somewhere in the hay and Anna whispered close to me not to answer or say anything. I obeyed her.

The sleigh started off. I heard the horses thumping in the snow and the harness bells falling into a steady jingling. Lying on my back, I looked into the night. Stars filled the sky and a white glare hung over the housetops. The street was silent. I could no longer see the snow-covered houses with their lighted windows. My nose filled with the fresh smell of snow and the barn smells of hay and horse blankets, I lay, listening to the different sounds—the harness bells and the snow crunching under the runners.

The stillness of this winter's night was as intense as the storm that had raged for three days. I felt that all the wind and snow there was had blown themselves out forever and that the night as far as the highest star had been emptied by the storm. This emptiness as I lay looking into it was like being hypnotized. It was something to run out into, to fly up into, as the snowfall had been. I began to want to see further, and the star-filled sky that had seemed so vast a few minutes ago now didn't seem vast enough.

I had almost forgotten about Anna when I felt a now familiar warmth press against me. She had moved closer, as if joggled by the sleigh. I held my breath waiting for her to order me to move away and give her room, but she was silent.

My hand at my side touched her fingers. Now I forgot the sky and the great sprinkle of stars that seemed like a thin, far-away snowfall that had stopped moving. The night, the glare of snow, the jingling harness bells died away; only my fingers were alive.

When I had looked at her hand tapping gently on the lapboard, it had seemed strange, and the thought of touching it somehow disillusioning. But now under the horse blankets, hidden in the hay, this hand seemed more breathing and mysterious and familiar than anything about her. I lay unable to move closer to it, our fingertips barely touching. I grew dizzy wishing to reach her hand, but I felt as powerless to move toward it as to fly.

The minutes passed. Two of the Joneses started singing. The thump of the horses, the jingling of the sleighbells, and the crunching of the snow under the runners seemed part of this soft singing. I too wished to sing, to stand up suddenly in this sweeping-along sleigh and bellow at the silent night.

Then the fingers for which I had been wishing until I was dizzy seemed to start walking under the horse blankets, seemed to be running toward me in the warm hay. They came as far as my hand, closed around it, and I felt the throb of their tips against my palm. The night turned into a dream. I opened my eyes to the wide sprinkle of stars and a mist seemed to have come over them. The snow-covered hills over which we were gliding sparkled behind a mist, and suddenly the night into which I was looking lost its hours. It stretched away without time as if it were not something that was passing like our sleigh over the snow, but a star-filled winter's night that would never change and never move.

Lying beside Anna, her hand in mine, with the sleigh now flying in a whirl of snow down the white hill, I thought this night would never end.

THE SORCERER'S EYE

by Howard Nemerov

AROUND THE CASTLE where I lived with my parents was
a moat, half overgrown with weeds, where wild birds
waded and swam. A corridor, which I liked to think was
secret, led to a door at the water's edge, and there I used to
go, against my father's absolute command, to meet the girl
from outside. We spoke across the water.

"What is that you wear on the string around your neck?"
she asked me once. I drew it from my shirt, a golden spoon
it was, and showed it to her.

"Why a golden spoon?" she asked.

"Oh," I said, "it is something that happened long ago, a
kind of family joke, though not a very good one. You
wouldn't be interested."

"You're a sad boy, aren't you?" said she. "Do they really
joke, in your family? Tell me."

"When I was little," I said, "my father once told me, he
seemed angry about it, that I had been born with a golden
spoon in my mouth. That puzzled me, since I didn't know it
was a proverb, and I tried to think what it was like to be
born, and why one would have a golden spoon in one's
mouth at that time, and finally, seeing that my father really
meant something, which it made him angry to mean, I
started to cry. My mother then, to turn it into a joke, took
a real golden spoon from the dinner table, tapped me on
the shoulder with it, and said I was her knight of the golden
spoon. So I have kept the spoon."

The girl smiled. She was dressed in black rags, and so
beautiful.

"You love your mother, don't you?" she said.

"She is sick," I replied. "She lies on a sofa all day, and has little heart-shaped white pastilles, for her heart ailment. She reads novels, and sometimes I read them to her, though Father does not like me to be reading novels."

"There's a great lot your father doesn't like."

"He doesn't like at all for me to meet you and talk to you."

"I know," said she. "We're both lonely."

"I am so lonely," said I. "For I read in books about how people live, out in the world, and meet others, and make friends, and love another. I love you, I think."

"I love you," she said, "but it would be better not to talk of that."

"Because of your father?" I asked.

"Because of him, yes."

"I know about your father," I said, "for my father told me the tale on my eighteenth birthday, only a while ago. I have even seen your father, through the telescope in the tower room. He sits in the woods, in a clearing in the woods, a mile away. He sits on a throne of sorts, I think, and stares at our castle all the time. He is a sorcerer, isn't he, a kind of wizard?"

"He is," said she.

"And my father is frightened of him," I went on, "for he built this castle of ours by magic, before I was born, and my father fears that if he is offended he may tear it down, also by magic."

"That's true, he could," she said. "Your father must have been in terrible trouble, to need my father's help."

"My father used to live in the world," I said. "He was a captain in one of the great regiments, and he had epaulets of silver, high boots, silver spurs. But he lived too well, and gambled, and was in debt. One night, when he was drunk and losing everything, he bet against a brother officer and on his side the wager was that this man, if he won, might spend a night with my mother."

"That was a bad thing to do," said the girl.

"It was," I said, "for he lost. Everyone knew then that it

was not only a bad bet but an impossible one, and they left him alone until sunrise, with a pistol on the table. My father was to shoot himself because of his dishonor; that was the understanding, in the regiment. But instead he went out and walked in the streets of the city until, near dawn, he met your father, who brought him into the deep forest, far away, and raised him up this fine castle which you see —all by a look of the eye he did this, and by a gesture of the hand."

"My father has a great and terrible power," the girl said. "There was a condition."

"The condition was simply this," I replied, "that we live here, that we never go outside."

"You are safe, at any rate."

"Yes," I said, "we are safe enough. But my father is unhappy, and that makes us all unhappy. He is unhappy because, I think, he believes still that he might somehow have got out of his desperate position and gone on to a grand career, and because my mother is ill and not much of a companion to him, and because she despises him, having never forgiven the wager. Finally," I said with some hesitation, "because he suspects, and fears, that after all his fellow officer might have taken advantage of his winning, on that night, so I would be not my father's child but his. About this, he has never asked my mother, as fearing her reply, as not wanting the burden of the knowledge, I don't know."

We were silent. The waters of the moat glittered between us. Behind me the castle stood towering in courses of great blocks of stone, behind her the trees flickered their green leaves in the light wind and the sunshine.

"I never knew my mother," said the girl at last.

"I'm sorry for that," said I.

"Nor have I been in the world," she said. "I am as much a prisoner as you are, and perhaps my father is as much a prisoner as yours. The keeper is always bound to his charge, so neither can be free."

"I should like to go into the world," I said, "but only if you would go with me."

"My father has two eyes," she said, musingly, and as if not replying at all, "of which the right one, of flesh and blood, is the eye of action, and the left one, a glass orb, is the eye of thought. With the one, he does; with the other, he knows."

"That is a strange division," I said, "and yet, after all, quite appropriate in its way."

"I have been thinking," she said, "that as my father's eyes are fixed upon the castle, so that you and I are beneath his notice, we might go together, one time, and come up behind him, and you with your golden spoon could quickly remove an eye—"

"But that would be terrible," said I, "in itself and in its consequences."

"Terrible, how?" asked the girl. "I do not love my father."

"Nor I mine," I replied, "though I should be sorry to lose my mother. But the castle would fall."

"Not if you removed the glass eye," she said. "It would not hurt him to lose it, since it is glass, since it is the eye of knowledge he would never know he had lost it, so that it follows, surely, that he must keep the eye of action turned, as always, upon the castle, to keep it as it is, in being."

"That's true," I said, beginning to be fascinated with the idea. "But dangerous."

"You are afraid?" she asked, smiling again.

"I have never been afraid," I said, somewhat sternly, but yet not pridefully, for the fact was that my existence until this time had magically excluded the awareness of fear.

"When it is done," she said, "we shall go out into the world, away from castle and forest, and I promise to love you for as long as you will love me."

"I will do it for that promise," I said. "I will do it for you."

"Tonight," she said, "meet me here again, and I will lead you where he sits."

So we parted, agreeing to meet in the hour before dawn.

2

"You've been seeing that girl again," said my father during the course of the evening.

"No, sir," I said, looking him steadily in the eye. I thought that he had not seen me down there by the moat, but said this simply from a sad propensity, almost a wish, to know the worst, at all times, about everything.

"I hope you are not lying to me," he said, frowning. "You know how I regard a lie."

He had come to a stop facing me, but now he resumed his usual occupation of pacing the long hall, with his hands locked behind him. Whenever he turned toward me, however, he thought of something else to say.

"It's for your good, as well as mine, that I warn you" was one of these remarks. And another was "Don't imagine I shan't know what you do." And another: "I don't like to have to keep an eye perpetually on what my own son is up to; but I will, I will if it is necessary, make no mistake about that."

My silence during all this was meant to be respectful, though it was also shamefaced because of the lie; it seemed merely to provoke him further, so that at last he came to a definite halt in front of me, but spoke rather to the ceiling, or the walls, than to me.

"What difference does it make? What can I keep? What have I to defend? A merciless bargain. Are you my son? Are you?"

"I don't know," I said, though he still seemed to be talking at random rather than to me. "I cannot know if you don't, sir."

"Ah, I know you'll do as you please," he said roughly, and then, "If you see that child once more—once more— let me tell you, lad—"

"Yes, Father," said I meekly but by no means humbly.

"I will . . . I will . . . ah, what will I?" he rather groaned than said, and stalked away leaving me there. I felt sad for him in his merciless bargain, but undisturbed in my resolve. The bargain had not been mine, and perhaps what I was about to do had, in some way, been included in the pact to begin with, before I was born. He was an elegant, lean man, my father, still young-looking, and I had always thought him strong. But I now saw that his strength was of the sort which is purely for display and is always defeated in action; that is why it could continue to look like strength, because there was really for him, poor man, no world in which he might expend it.

My mother, though, was the image of a continuously victorious weakness. Fragile and lovely, with her romances and her little medicated confections for the heart, she lay there year after year, not so much indomitable—that was the quality she had lived on, and used up—as simply undefeated. I told her nothing, that night; but she felt a foreboding.

"Something . . . something . . . will happen, soon."

"Oh, Mother," I said quite boldly, "all will be well, you will live in your castle still. Whatever happens, trust your knight of the golden spoon, who will never let anything bad happen to you." For I believed at this time that I was going to be their savior as well as my own. I should free myself, and go into the world, and love another, while they would possess their fine castle unconditionally, when I had removed the glass eye of knowledge from the sorcerer's head, so that it might never revoke the action of the other eye which kept the castle standing. So all would be well, with them and with me.

I reassured my mother, and then for a while read to her, as I sometimes did, from the novel she happened to be reading at the time. Because she read these novels far more when I was not there than had them read when I was, my impression of the life in them was flickering and discontinuous: someone would be happy at one reading, on the point of suicide at the next, married at the next, then dead, and so on; also, different people would have entered while I was away, and the people I knew from previous readings would have disappeared; I never knew, even, when one novel left off and a quite different one replaced it.

In the chapter I read that night a man abandoned his wife and child, on account of something he had done which doubtless had been described in an earlier part, but which I knew nothing of. As he left the house at night, he stood at the end of the street to look back once at the little light above the door, emblem of a happiness lost and a security decayed, so that the author, a woman, was moved to exclaim to us readers, "The gleam of that lantern would illuminate his mind for many years," and, an instant later, "how far that little lantern threw its beams!" expressions which, sentimental as they may have been in that place, I have been unable to forget. At the time, however, I affected to regard them slightly, and may even have read these phrases with a tone of mockery, for my mother said to me, as I bent to kiss her good night and, as I thought, goodbye, that when one day I had gone into the world and married and knew what it was to be a father, I should perceive the bitter truth at the heart of those words which I now found merely sugary.

3

Before dawn, by the black waters of the moat, without a moon to silver them, I stood shivering. At her low, long call I dived as deep and far as I could, felt for an instant the weeds cling and grasp about me, and came up at her feet. We set off roundabout through the forest, she holding my hand and leading the way with a great certainty, though nothing could be seen.

"You remember what you have to do?" she whispered once. I whispered that I did, though really what went through my head was scarcely a thought, so much as the mere image of my bending over that high and crooked shoulder from behind and suddenly, violently, digging with my golden spoon.

We reached the glade in the forest at first light, when a few birds were beginning to cry out. The girl, my girl, was pale, pale as stone in this gray light, and, though I was

not afraid, something of what fear was began to make itself
known to me through her hand, sweating but coldly sweating, which clutched mine always more tightly as we crept
into the clearing behind the old man's high throne, above
which reared back his great shoulders cloaked in black
and his massive, steady head, which never moved.

"Now!" she whispered, letting go my hand and pushing
me out toward the figure in the glade. I took the spoon,
tearing the cord which tied it to my neck, ran forward, and
leaped up, grasping that head by its white hair so that it fell
back while with my other hand I did with the spoon what I
had come to do.

Oh, I saw his face at that instant, and it was terrible, and
I knew now how to be afraid. The air was split by his one
cry of anguish, which endured while I dropped to the
ground and began to run. The girl caught me by the hand
again; in my other hand I held the spoon, and in the spoon
was held the eye, and his mighty voice screamed behind us
as we ran, "I know you! I know you!"

"Not that way," that girl began to bicker at me, "not
that way, that leads back to the castle."

"I know," said I. "I took the wrong eye."

"I know you!" screamed the voice behind us. "I know
what you have done."

As we ran through the forest the sun rose before us, and
its red and gold light flickered through the leaves in a
rhythm like that beaten by my brain: I know you, I know
you. The eye stuck to the spoon, the spoon was clenched
in my hand. Now I was the leader, and I was afraid, while
the girl tagged on behind me, and the great voice of agony
wakened the forest and the whole world.

"I can't run any more," she began to cry out after a
time, and when despite my terrible impatience and fear I
turned to attend to her weakness I saw no beautiful young
girl, whose white flesh peeped at the shoulder through her
rags, and whom I loved, but a thickened, sallow, blotched
creature dressed in a somewhat elegant gown which was,
however, badly ripped and stained.

"I can't go on any more," she cried chokingly, and

sagged to the ground. As I took up my flight again I heard her for a time begging me not to leave her, but I could not stop.

The castle, when I reached it, was a silent ruin. The moat had dried up, and in the dry ravine where it had been was a tangle of bushes and vines and tall grass. Great trees had fallen, it seemed centuries ago, against what was left of the castle walls, brought low now and with the contours of the great stones softened by moss and lichen. One of these trees I was able to use as a bridge, and in a moment stood atop a heap of marble slabs mingled with granite blocks. Before me, in a kind of pit formed by the inward collapse of battlements, my mother sat on a stone, with my father standing beside her. He held her by the hand. I saw that they were old, quite old, and wrinkled, with dry, papery faces. And I was frightened anew, even before my father cried out to me, in a shrill voice, "What have you done? Monster, what have you done?" And my mother said, in a dull voice as though she cared for nothing in the world, "What is that in your hand?"

I looked at my hand, at the spoon, at the eye which quivered there like a jelly. In that instant I knew all the fear my childhood had been denied, all the fear, I think, of children all over the world when in their sinfulness and shame they stand before the mighty parents whom they are bidden to destroy. And as though by this means I might rid myself of the evidence of my guilt, I raised the spoon to my mouth and swallowed down the eye.

"What's done is done," I said to them sternly. "Come, we shall leave here at once."

And that is what we did, with nothing in our hands except my golden spoon. My parents opposed me no more, and we walked out into the forest, in the heat of the day, where I could still hear as it were the leaves of the trees shaking in slight sound: "I know you!" And this great forest, which from the castle had once seemed of illimitable extent in every direction, proved to go on for a few miles only. By midafternoon we had come out on a highway, with rails sunk in it, and on the rails was what I later understood to be a tram car. Of course, as we had no money, it was necessary to walk. And when, some time later, we came into the city, it was hard at first to find food and lodging. But I was now the owner—despite himself!—of the eye of power and action, and it is enough to say that I soon found work, which enabled me to provide for my parents while they lived.

It was not long. My mother was very shortly afterward taken by a fatal attack, and then my father, stealing money from me in order to do so, bought a pistol and with it one night blew out his brains, just as though he were a gallant young captain still, and nineteen years had never passed.

Since then, I have gone about my business in the world, preferring travel to residence, being, as you might say, an *entrepreneur*. I have done quite well with my life, following my many concernments from one town to another, living always in hotels, a long succession of them so that they seem to become one in my memory, with their marbles and potted palms and ancient elevators of open grillework in which the passengers arise and descend like angels in trousers and spats or in tea gowns and pumps. All those towns seem a single town in the flickering rhythm of my brain, Nineveh, perhaps, that great city which the Lord spared, as I read once, although there were therein so many persons that could not discern between their right hand and their left hand.

I have never married. And I have kept my golden spoon, for a watch charm. I used to eat my breakfast egg with it, but gave that up many years back as being bravado. And somewhere, in a small clearing in my busy brain, the black-robed magician sits still in his high chair and cries out in an anguish undiminished by time or by his impotence that he knows me, he knows me.

TOMORROW AND TOMORROW
AND SO FORTH

by John Updike

WHIRLING, talking, 11D began to enter Room 109. From the quality of their excitement Mark Prosser guessed it would rain. He had been teaching high school for three years, yet his students still impressed him; they were such sensitive animals. They reacted so infallibly to merely barometric pressure.

In the doorway, Brute Young paused while little Barry Snyder giggled at his elbow. Barry's stagy laugh rose and fell, dipping down toward some vile secret that had to be tasted and retasted, then soaring artificially to proclaim that he, little Barry, shared such a secret with the school's fullback. Being Brute's stooge was precious to Barry. The fullback paid no attention to him; he twisted his neck to stare at something not yet coming through the door. He yielded heavily to the procession pressing him forward.

Right under Prosser's eyes, like a murder suddenly appearing in an annalistic frieze of kings and queens, someone stabbed a girl in the back with a pencil. She ignored the assault saucily. Another hand yanked out Geoffrey Langer's shirt-tail. Geoffrey, a bright student, was uncertain whether to laugh it off or defend himself with anger, and made a weak, half-turning gesture of compromise, wearing an expression of distant arrogance that Prosser instantly coördinated with feelings of fear he used to have. All along the line, in the glitter of key chains and the acute angles of turned-back shirt cuffs, an electricity was expressed which simple weather couldn't generate.

Mark wondered if today Gloria Angstrom wore that sweater, an ember-pink angora, with very brief sleeves.

The virtual sleevelessness was the disturbing factor: the exposure of those two serene arms to the air, white as thighs against the delicate wool.

His guess was correct. A vivid pink patch flashed through the jiggle of arms and shoulders as the final knot of youngsters entered the room.

"Take your seats," Mr. Prosser said. "Come on. Let's go."

Most obeyed, but Peter Forrester, who had been at the center of the group around Gloria, still lingered in the doorway with her, finishing some story, apparently determined to make her laugh or gasp. When she did gasp, he tossed his head with satisfaction. His orange hair bobbed. Redheads are all alike, Mark thought, with their white eyelashes and pale puffy faces and thyroid eyes, their mouths always twisted with preposterous self-confidence. Bluffers, the whole bunch.

When Gloria, moving in a considered, stately way, had taken her seat, and Peter had swerved into his, Mr. Prosser said, "Peter Forrester."

"Yes?" Peter rose, scrabbling through his book for the right place.

"Kindly tell the class the exact meaning of the words 'Tomorrow, and tomorrow, and tomorrow/Creeps in this petty pace from day to day.' "

Peter glanced down at the high-school edition of *Macbeth* lying open on his desk. One of the duller girls tittered expectantly from the back of the room. Peter was popular with the girls; girls that age had minds like moths.

"Peter. With your book shut. We have all memorized this passage for today. Remember?" The girl in the back of the room squealed in delight. Gloria laid her own book face-open on her desk, where Peter could see it.

Peter shut his book with a bang and stared into Gloria's. "Why," he said at last, "I think it means pretty much what it says."

"Which is?"

"Why, that tomorrow is something we often think about. It creeps into our conversation all the time. We couldn't make any plans without thinking about tomorrow."

"I see. Then you would say that Macbeth is here refer-
ring to the, the date-book aspect of life?"

Geoffrey Langer laughed, no doubt to please Mr. Prosser. For a moment, he *was* pleased. Then he realized he
had been playing for laughs at a student's expense.

His paraphrase had made Peter's reading of the lines
seem more ridiculous than it was. He began to retract.
"I admit—"

But Peter was going on; redheads never know when to
quit. "Macbeth means that if we quit worrying about tomorrow, and just lived for today, we could appreciate all
the wonderful things that are going on under our noses."

Mark considered this a moment before he spoke. He
would not be sarcastic. "Uh, without denying that there is
truth in what you say, Peter, do you think it likely that
Macbeth, in his situation, would be expressing such"—he
couldn't help himself—"such sunny sentiments?"

Geoffrey laughed again. Peter's neck reddened; he studied
the floor. Gloria glared at Mr. Prosser, the anger in her
face clearly meant for him to see.

Mark hurried to undo his mistake. "Don't misunderstand
me, please," he told Peter. "I don't have all the answers
myself. But it seems to me the whole speech, down to
'Signifying nothing,' is saying that life is—well, a *fraud*.
Nothing wonderful about it."

"Did Shakespeare really think that?" Geoffrey Langer
asked, a nervous quickness pitching his voice high.

Mark read into Geoffrey's question his own adolescent
premonitions of the terrible truth. The attempt he must
make was plain. He told Peter he could sit down and
looked through the window toward the steadying sky. The
clouds were gaining intensity. "There is," Mr. Prosser
slowly began, "much darkness in Shakespeare's work, and
no play is darker than *Macbeth*. The atmosphere is poison-
ous, oppressive. One critic has said that in this play,
humanity suffocates." This was too fancy.

"In the middle of his career, Shakespeare wrote plays
about men like Hamlet and Othello and Macbeth—men

who aren't allowed by their society, or bad luck, or some minor flaw in themselves, to become the great men they might have been. Even Shakespeare's comedies of this period deal with a world gone sour. It is as if he had seen through the bright, bold surface of his earlier comedies and histories and had looked upon something terrible. It frightened him, just as some day it may frighten some of you." In his determination to find the right words, he had been staring at Gloria, without meaning to. Embarrassed, she nodded, and, realizing what had happened, he smiled at her.

He tried to make his remarks gentler, even diffident. "But then I think Shakespeare sensed a redeeming truth. His last plays are serene and symbolical, as if he had pierced through the ugly facts and reached a realm where the facts are again beautiful. In this way, Shakespeare's total work is a more complete image of life than that of any other writer, except perhaps for Dante, an Italian poet who wrote several centuries earlier." He had been taken far from the Macbeth soliloquy. Other teachers had been happy to tell him how the kids made a game of getting him talking. He looked toward Geoffrey. The boy was doodling on his tablet, indifferent. Mr. Prosser concluded, "The last play Shakespeare wrote is an extraordinary poem called *The Tempest*. Some of you may want to read it for your next book reports—the ones due May 10th. It's a short play."

The class had been taking a holiday. Barry Snyder was snicking BBs off the blackboard and glancing over at Brute Young to see if he noticed. "Once more, Barry," Mr. Prosser said, "and out you go." Barry blushed, and grinned to cover the blush, his eyeballs sliding toward Brute. The dull girl in the rear of the room was putting on lipstick. "Put that away, Alice," Mr. Prosser commanded. She giggled and obeyed. Sejak, the Polish boy who worked nights, was asleep at his desk, his cheek white with pressure against the varnished wood, his mouth sagging sidewise. Mr. Prosser had an impulse to let him sleep. But the impulse might not be true kindness, but just the self-congratulatory, kindly pose in which he sometimes discovered himself. Besides, one breach of discipline encouraged others. He strode down the aisle and shook Sejak awake. Then he turned his attention to the mumble growing at the front of the room.

Peter Forrester was whispering to Gloria, trying to make her laugh. The girl's face, though, was cool and solemn, as if a thought had been provoked in her head. Perhaps at least *she* had been listening to what Mr. Prosser had been saying. With a bracing sense of chivalrous intercession, Mark said, "Peter. I gather from this noise that you have something to add to your theories."

Peter responded courteously. "No, sir. I honestly don't understand the speech. Please, sir, what *does* it mean?"

This candid admission and odd request stunned the class. Every white, round face, eager, for once, to learn, turned toward Mark. He said, "I don't know. I was hoping *you* would tell *me*."

In college, when a professor made such a remark, it was with grand effect. The professor's humility, the necessity for creative interplay between teacher and student were dramatically impressed upon the group. But to 11D, ignorance in an instructor was as wrong as a hole in a roof. It was as if he had held forty strings pulling forty faces taut toward him and then had slashed the strings. Heads waggled, eyes dropped, voices buzzed. Some of the discipline problems, like Peter Forrester, smirked signals to one another.

"Quiet!" Mr. Prosser shouted. "All of you. Poetry isn't arithmetic. There's no single right answer. I don't want to force my impression on you, even if I *have* had much more experience with literature." He made this last clause very loud and distinct, and some of the weaker students seemed reassured. "I know none of *you* want that," he told them.

Whether or not they believed him, they subsided, somewhat. Mark judged he could safely reassume his human-among-humans attitude again. He perched on the edge of the desk and leaned forward beseechingly. "Now, honestly. Don't any of you have some personal feelings about the lines that you would like to share with the class and me?"

One hand, with a flowered handkerchief balled in it, unsteadily rose. "Go ahead, Teresa," Mr. Prosser said encouragingly. She was a timid, clumsy girl whose mother was a Jehovah's Witness.

"It makes me think of cloud shadows," Teresa said.

Geoffrey Langer laughed. "Don't be rude, Geoff," Mr. Prosser said sideways, softly, before throwing his voice forward: "Thank you, Teresa. I think that's an interesting and valid impression. Cloud movement has something in it of the slow, monotonous rhythm one feels in the line 'Tomorrow, and tomorrow, and tomorrow.' It's a very gray line, isn't it, class?" No one agreed or disagreed.

Beyond the windows actual clouds were bunching rapidly, and erratic sections of sunlight slid around the room. Gloria's arm, crooked gracefully above her head, turned gold. "Gloria?" Mr. Prosser asked.

She looked up from something on her desk with a face of sullen radiance. "I think what Teresa said was very good," she said, glaring in the direction of Geoffrey Langer. Geoffrey chuckled defiantly. "And I have a question. What does 'petty pace' mean?"

"It means the trivial day-to-day sort of life that, say, a bookkeeper or a bank clerk leads. Or a schoolteacher," he added, smiling.

She did not smile back. Thought wrinkles irritated her perfect brow. "But Macbeth has been fighting wars, and killing kings, and being a king himself, and all," she pointed out.

"Yes, but it's just these acts Macbeth is condemning as 'nothing.' Can you see that?"

Gloria shook her head. "Another thing I worry about —isn't it silly for Macbeth to be talking to himself right in the middle of this war, with his wife just dead, and all?"

"I don't think so, Gloria. No matter how fast events happen, thought is faster."

His answer was weak; everyone knew it, even if Gloria hadn't mused, supposedly to herself, but in a voice the entire class could hear, "It seems so *stupid*."

Mark winced, pierced by the awful clarity with which his students saw him. Through their eyes, how queer he looked, with his long hands, and his horn-rimmed glasses, and his hair never slicked down, all wrapped up in "literature," where, when things get rough, the king mumbles a poem nobody understands. The delight Mr. Prosser took in such crazy junk made not only his good sense but his masculinity a matter of doubt. It was gentle of them not to laugh him out of the room. He looked down and rubbed his fingertips together, trying to erase the chalk dust. The class noise sifted into unnatural quiet. "It's getting late," he said finally. "Let's start the recitations of the memorized passage. Bernard Amilson, you begin."

Bernard had trouble enunciating, and his rendition began " 'T'mau 'n' t'mau 'n' t'mau.' " It was reassuring, the extent to which the class tried to repress its laughter. Mr. Prosser wrote "A" in his marking book opposite Bernard's name. He always gave Bernard A on recitations, despite the school nurse, who claimed there was nothing organically wrong with the boy's mouth.

It was the custom, cruel but traditional, to deliver recitations from the front of the room. Alice, when her turn came, was reduced to a helpless state by the first funny face Peter Forrester made at her. Mark let her hang up there a good minute while her face ripened to cherry redness, and at last forgave her. She may try it later. Many of the youngsters knew the passage gratifyingly well, though there was a tendency to leave out the line "To the last syllable of recorded time" and to turn "struts and frets" into "frets and struts" or simply "struts and struts." Even Sejak, who couldn't have looked at the passage before he came to class, got through it as far as "And then is heard no more."

Geoffrey Langer showed off, as he always did, by interrupting his own recitation with bright questions. " 'Tomorrow, and tomorrow, and tomorrow,' " he said, " 'creeps in'—shouldn't that be 'creep in,' Mr. Prosser?"

"It is 'creeps.' The trio is in effect singular. Go on." Mr.

Prosser was tired of coddling Langer. If you let them, these smart students will run away with the class. "Without the footnotes."

" 'Creep*sss* in this petty pace from day to day, to the last syllable of recorded time, and all our yesterdays have lighted fools the way to dusty death. Out, out—' "

"No, no!" Mr. Prosser jumped out of his chair. "This is poetry. Don't mushmouth it! Pause a little after 'fools.' " Geoffrey looked genuinely startled this time, and Mark himself did not quite understand his annoyance and, mentally turning to see what was behind him, seemed to glimpse in the humid undergrowth the two stern eyes of the indignant look Gloria had thrown Geoffrey. He glimpsed himself in the absurd position of acting as Gloria's champion in her private war with this intelligent boy. He sighed apologetically. "Poetry is made up of lines," he began, turning to the class. Gloria was passing a note to Peter Forrester.

The rudeness of it! To pass notes during a scolding that she herself had caused! Mark caged in his hand the girl's frail wrist and ripped the note from her fingers. He read it to himself, letting the class see he was reading it, though he despised such methods of discipline. The note went:

> Pete—I think you're *wrong* about Mr. Prosser. I think he's wonderful and I get a lot out of his class. He's heavenly with poetry. I think I love him. I really do *love* him. So there.

Mr. Prosser folded the note once and slipped it into his side coat pocket. "See me after class, Gloria," he said. Then, to Geoffrey, "Let's try it again. Begin at the beginning."

While the boy was reciting the passage, the buzzer sounded the end of the period. It was the last class of the day. The room quickly emptied, except for Gloria. The noise of lockers slamming open and books being thrown against metal and shouts drifted in.

"Who has a car?"

"Lend me a cig, pig."

"We can't have practice in this slop."

Mark hadn't noticed exactly when the rain started, but it was coming down fast now. He moved around the room with the window pole, closing windows and pulling down shades. Spray bounced in on his hands. He began to talk to Gloria in a crisp voice that, like his device of shutting the windows, was intended to protect them both from embarrassment.

"About note passing." She sat motionless at her desk in the front of the room, her short, brushed-up hair like a cool torch. From the way she sat, her naked arms folded at her breasts and her shoulders hunched, he felt she was chilly. "It is not only rude to scribble when a teacher is talking, it is stupid to put one's words down on paper, where they look much more foolish than they might have sounded if spoken." He leaned the window pole in its corner and walked toward his desk.

"And about love. 'Love' is one of those words that illustrate what happens to an old, overworked language. These days, with movie stars and crooners and preachers and psychiatrists all pronouncing the word, it's come to mean nothing but a vague fondness for something. In this sense, I love the rain, this blackboard, these desks, you. It means nothing, you see, whereas once the word signified a quite explicit thing—a desire to share all you own and are with someone else. It is time we coined a new word to mean that, and when you think up the word *you* want to use, I suggest that you be economical with it. Treat it as something you can spend only once—if not for your own sake, for the good of the language." He walked over to his own desk and dropped two pencils on it, as if to say, "That's all."

"I'm sorry," Gloria said.

Rather surprised, Mr. Prosser said, "Don't be."

"But you don't understand."

"Of course I don't. I probably never did. At your age, I was like Geoffrey Langer."

"I bet you weren't." The girl was almost crying; he was sure of that.

"Come on, Gloria. Run along. Forget it." She slowly cradled her books between her bare arm and her sweater, and left the room with that melancholy shuffling teen-age gait, so that her body above her thighs seemed to float over the desks.

What was it, Mark asked himself, these kids were after? What did they want? Glide, he decided, the quality of glide. To slip along, always in rhythm, always cool, the little wheels humming under you, going nowhere special. If Heaven existed, that's the way it would be there. "He's heavenly with poetry." They loved the word. Heaven was in half their songs.

"Christ, he's humming," Strunk, the physical ed teacher, had come into the room without Mark's noticing. Gloria had left the door ajar.

"Ah," Mark said, "a fallen angel, full of grit."

"What the hell makes you so happy?"

"I'm not happy, I'm just serene. I don't know why you don't appreciate me."

"Say." Strunk came up an aisle with a disagreeably effeminate waddle, pregnant with gossip. "Did you hear about Murchison?"

"No." Mark mimicked Strunk's whisper.

"He got the pants kidded off him today."

"Oh dear."

Strunk started to laugh, as he always did before beginning a story. "You know what a goddam lady's man he thinks he is?"

"You bet," Mark said, although Strunk said that about every male member of the faculty.

"You have Gloria Angström, don't you?"

"You bet."

"Well, this morning Murky intercepts a note she was writing, and the note says what a damn neat guy she thinks Murchison is and how she *loves* him!" Strunk waited for Mark to say something, and then, when he didn't, continued, "You could see he was tickled pink. But —get this—it turns out at lunch that the same damn thing happened to Freyburg in history yesterday!" Strunk laughed and cracked his knuckles viciously. "The girl's too dumb to have thought it up herself. We all think it was Peter Forrester's idea."

"Probably was," Mark agreed. Strunk followed him out to his locker, describing Murchison's expression when Freyburg (in all innocence, mind you) told what had happened to him.

Mark turned the combination of his locker, 18-24-3. "Would you excuse me, Dave?" he said. "My wife's in town waiting."

Strunk was too thick to catch Mark's anger. "I got to get over to the gym. Can't take the little darlings outside in the rain; their mommies'll write notes to teacher." He clattered down the hall and wheeled at the far end, shouting, "Now don't tell You-know-who!"

Mr. Prosser took his coat from the locker and shrugged it on. He placed his hat upon his head. He fitted his rubbers over his shoes, pinching his fingers painfully, and lifted his umbrella off the hook. He thought of opening it right there in the vacant hall, as a kind of joke, and decided not to. The girl had been almost crying; he was sure of that.

AH, THE UNIVERSITY

by John Collier

JUST OUTSIDE LONDON there lived an old father who dearly loved his only son. Accordingly, when the boy was a youngster of some eighteen years, the old man sent for him and, with a benevolent glimmer of his horn-rimmed spectacles, said, "Well, Jack, you are now done with school. No doubt you are looking forward to going to the university."

"Yes, Dad, I am," said the son.

"You show good judgment," said the father. "The best years of one's whole life are unquestionably those which are spent at the university. Apart from the vast honeycomb of learning, the mellow voices of the professors, the venerable gray buildings, and the atmosphere of culture and refinement, there is the delight of being in possession of a comfortable allowance."

"Yes, Dad," said the son.

"Rooms of one's own," continued the father, "little dinners to one's friends, endless credit with the tradespeople, pipes, cigars, claret, Burgundy, clothes."

"Yes, Dad," said the son.

"There are exclusive little clubs," said the old man, "all sorts of sports, May Weeks, theatricals, balls, parties, rags, binges, scaling of walls, dodging of proctors, fun of every conceivable description."

"Yes! Yes, Dad!" cried the son.

"Certainly nothing in the world is more delightful than being at the university," said the father. "The springtime of life! Pleasure after pleasure! The world seems a whole dozen oysters, each with a pearl in it. Ah, the university! However, I'm not going to send you there."

"Then why the hell do you go on so about it?" said poor Jack.

"I did so in order that you might not think I was carelessly underestimating the pleasures I must call upon you to renounce," said his father. "You see, Jack, my health is not of the best; nothing but champagne agrees with me, and if I smoke a second-rate cigar, I get a vile taste in my mouth. My expenses have mounted abominably and I shall have very little to leave to you, yet my dearest wish is to see you in a comfortable way of life."

"If that is your wish, you might gratify it by sending me to the university," said Jack.

"We must think of the future," said his father. "You will have your living to earn, and in a world where culture is the least marketable of assets. Unless you are to be a schoolmaster or a curate, you will gain no great advantage from the university."

"Then what am I to be?" the young man asked.

"I read only a little while ago," said his father, "the following words, which flashed like sudden lightning upon the gloom in which I was considering your future: 'Most players are weak.' These words came from a little brochure upon the delightful and universally popular game of poker. It is a game which is played for counters, commonly called chips, and each of these chips represents an agreeable sum of money."

"Do you mean that I am to be a card-sharper?" cried the son.

"Nothing of the sort," replied the old man promptly. "I am asking you to be strong, Jack. I am asking you to show initiative, individuality. Why learn what everyone else is learning? You, my dear boy, shall be the first to study poker as systematically as others study languages, science, mathematics, and so forth—the first to tackle it as a student. I have set aside a cosy little room with chair, table, and some completely new packs of cards. A bookshelf contains several standard works on the game, and a portrait of Machiavelli hangs above the mantelpiece."

The young man's protests were vain, so he set himself reluctantly to study. He worked hard, mastered the books, wore the spots off a hundred packs of cards, and at the end of the second year he set out into the world with his father's blessing and enough cash to sit in on a few games of penny ante.

After Jack left, the old man consoled himself with his glass of champagne and his first-rate cigar and those other little pleasures which are the solace of the old and the lonely. He was getting on very well with these when one day the telephone rang. It was an overseas call from Jack, whose existence the old man had all but forgotten.

"Hullo, Dad!" cried the son in tones of great excitement. "I'm in Paris, sitting in on a game of poker with some Americans."

"Good luck to you!" said the old man, preparing to hang up the receiver.

"Listen, Dad!" cried the son. "It's like this. Well—just for once I'm playing without any limit."

"Lord have mercy on you!" said the old man.

"There's two of them still in," said the son. "They've raised me fifty thousand dollars and I've already put up every cent I've got."

"I would rather," groaned the old man, "see a son of mine at the university than in such a situation."

"But I've got four kings!" cried the young man.

"You can be sure the others have aces or straight flushes," said the old man. "Back down, my poor boy. Go out and play for cigarette ends with the habitués of your rooming house."

"But listen, Dad!" cried the son. "This is a stud round, and nothing wild. I've seen an ace chucked in. I've seen all the tens and fives chucked in. There isn't a straight flush possible."

"Is that so?" cried the old man. "Never let it be said I didn't stand behind my boy. Hold everything. I'm coming to your assistance."

The son went back to the card table and begged his opponents to postpone matters until his father could arrive, and they, smiling at their cards, were only too willing to oblige him.

A couple of hours later the old man arrived by plane at Le Bourget, and shortly thereafter, he was standing beside the card table, rubbing his hands, smiling, affable, the light glinting merrily upon his horn-rimmed spectacles. He shook hands with the Americans and noted their prosperous appearances. "Now what have we here?" said he, sliding into his son's seat and fishing out his money.

"The bet," said one of the opponents, "stands at fifty thousand dollars. Seen by me. It's for you to see or raise."

"Or run," said the other.

"I trust my son's judgment," said the old man. "I shall raise fifty thousand dollars before I even glance at these cards in my hand." With that he pushed forward a hundred thousand dollars of his own money.

"I'll raise that hundred thousand dollars," said the first of his opponents.

"I'll stay and see," said the other.

The old man looked at his cards. His face turned several colours in rapid succession. A low and quavering groan burst from his lips and he was seen to hesitate for a long time, showing all the signs of an appalling inward struggle. At last he summoned up his courage and, pushing out his last hundred thousand (which represented all the cigars, champagne, and other little pleasures he had to look forward to), he licked his lips several times and said, "I'll see you."

"Four kings," said the first opponent, laying down his hand.

"Hell!" said the second. "Four queens."

"And I," moaned the old man, "have four knaves." With that he turned about and seized his son by the lapels of his jacket, shaking him as a terrier does a rat. "Curse the day," said he, "that I ever became the father of a damned fool!"

"I swear I thought they were kings," cried the young man.

"Don't you know that the 'v' is for valets?" said his father.

"Good God!" the son said. "I thought the 'v' was something to do with French kings. You know, Charles, Louis, V one, V two, V three. Oh, what a pity I was never at the university!"

"Go," said the old man. "Go there, or go to Hell or wherever you wish. Never let me see or hear from you again." And he stamped out of the room before his son or anyone else could say a word, even to tell him it was high-low stud they were playing and that the four knaves had won half the pot.

The young man, pocketing his share, mused that ignorance of every sort is deplorable, and, bidding his companions farewell, left Paris without further delay, and very soon he was entered at the university.